© 2008 McSweeney's Quarterly Concern, San Francisco, California. INTERNS & VOLUNTEERS: Jesse Nathan, Christopher Benz, Graham Weatherly, Alexandra Brown, Michael Zelenko, David Aloi, Candice Chan, Claire Donato, Peter Mack, Eva Tseng, Jessica Johnson, Ian MacLean, Anna Francesca Merlan, Michael Sisskin, Christina Rush, Diana Van Der Jagt, M. Rebekah Otto, Tanya Sirkin, Britta Ameel, Théophile Sersiron, Benjamin Jahn, Eliana Stein. ALSO HELPING: Alvaro Villanueva, Chris Ying, Michelle Quint, Greg Larson, Barb Bersche. COPY EDITORS: Domenick Ammirati, Oriana Leckert. EDITORS-AT-LARGE: Gabe Hudson, Lawrence Weschler, Sean Wilsey. WEBSITE: Chris Monks, Ed Page. OUTREACH: Angela Petrella, Darren Franich. CIRCULATION: Heidi Meredith. ASSOCIATE EDITOR/DESIGNER: Brian McMullen. MANAGING EDITOR: Jordan Bass. PUBLISHER: Eli Horowitz. EDITOR: Dave Eggers.

A NOTE ABOUT THE ART: The matchbox labels seen here, most of them Eastern European in origin, were collected by Jane McDevitt, a web designer living in the United Kingdom. Her website is www.maraid.co.uk.

It's Nice When Someone Is Excited to Hear from You

BRIAN BAISE

ROBUR

KONSUM-ZÜNDWARENWERK RIESA 2/65

I made a mistake a few years ago and took a job selling software on commission in Toledo, Ohio. I had been in San Francisco before that. Beautiful San Francisco! I can still see the golden hills in the distance!

I have no idea why I left. All my friends were there. We moved to California after college and took jobs in the industry. Stock options, free soda, ping-pong at work—the whole bit. This was about 1996. Things were just heating up, really. But I don't know. Maybe it started to disgust me after a while. Maybe the whole thing started to seem a little pathetic. So I took a flyer on a job offer from one of our clients in Toledo. Some people probably thought I was crazy—I'd never even been to Toledo. But most of my friends didn't know I was leaving—I didn't tell them. I wanted them to wake up one day and look around and wonder a bit. And frankly, I was relieved to never have to speak to them again. I really thought I despised them—the whole crew. I was glad to be gone.

A year later, the company folded. The guy who hired me—he moved to Hawaii. The Na Pali Coast, I heard, right above the breakers. Supposedly he took up body surfing. They said I could keep my accounts if I wanted and do with them what I might, but I'd have to work out of my apartment, and there wouldn't be any base salary. It was depressing as hell, to be perfectly honest. My apartment had these green walls and ceilings, and the rugs all had mold in them from the humidity. I had a balcony that overlooked the river, but the river was brown and slow and foul, and at night there was a certain kind of lizard fish that liked to climb up out of the water and slither around on the bank. You could see it from my balcony. The moonlight was always glistening off its wet, disgusting back.

Years managed to go by this way—the lizard fish, me, my stupid little software packages. I had one friend, a guy named Chaney. Almost literally, he was the only person I knew in the entire state of Ohio. I mean I recognized a neighbor or two, but his was the only phone number I had. The first time I met him—which was through business—he invited me to a club out in the sticks where for twenty bucks a woman would let you stick your finger in her pussy. He had a group of about four or five guys that he made me a part of. I never liked them as much as I liked Chaney—they all just wanted to *be* Chaney, it seemed like. They even dressed like him.

Usually we went to this one bar, called the Black Bar, which happened to be down the street from my apartment, right along the river. It wasn't exactly a strip club, but the waitresses didn't wear very much clothing. We went there just about every night of the week. It was called the Black Bar because everything in it was black, including the pool table. Even the windows were black. From the outside, it looked as if it had been burned out and condemned. There wasn't a sign or anything.

As it happened, I still had to go back to San Francisco every few months to try and drum up business, but I never saw anyone—any of my old friends. I don't know why, really. I mean, I thought about it a couple of times. I thought it might be fun to go out to dinner or something and catch up, to see how everyone was doing and all that. But I was getting the sense all the way from Ohio that a mutual resentment had built up between us. I mean, nobody had even tried to contact me—to find out where I was, or whether or not I was still alive.

Anyway, it wasn't even worth thinking about anymore. It was ancient history. When I came to town, I stayed in a corporate hotel on Market Street down by the water and ate dinner by myself. I had my meetings and then I got out of there. There was no reason to stick around. That part of San Francisco is depressing as hell at night. It's like a graveyard. Nobody's around, and they dim the lights, and the fog is always sneaking down the streets and around the buildings. If you stay up late enough, you find out that they bring in these tanker trucks to spray everything down—all the dirt and trash and grime. The only nice thing is that you can walk down the street and watch the lights breathing across the bay in Oakland, up in the hills. But even then the cars are banging and rattling on the bridge above you and usually it's so dark that you can't even see the water. I mean, you know it's there, because you can hear it washing up and down against the jetties, but you can't *see* it. It always feels as if you're just about to get murdered.

But then one time I called up Paul Lansky. It was about six o'clock in the evening, and I'd had a few drinks, I admit, and I was just sitting there in my hotel room, not doing anything. I don't know why I called him—I sort of just picked up the phone and dialed the number I still had in my head. He answered, too, and when I told him who it was, he got pretty excited, I could tell. It's nice when someone is excited to hear from you. It doesn't happen very often, but it's nice when it does. At first, he didn't even believe it *was* me—I mean he did, but in a sort of humorous way he pretended he didn't. I had to give him all sorts of biographical information before he finally dropped the charade. Then he said something that made me pretty angry for a moment: he said he didn't think he was ever going to hear from me again. I can't stand when people say that. He couldn't call me? People always think you should be the one calling them. I didn't say anything, though; I just let the comment slide. I said I'd been busy and that's why I hadn't called, which was a lie—I hadn't been doing anything other than hanging out with Chaney. And then I said I just wanted to see how he was doing—to see how life was turning out for him. He said life was turning out great for him, really great. That's great, I said. Then he wanted to know how I was doing. Great, I said. Excellent. Really excellent. Toledo—what a city! And right then I had this strange moment where I sort of observed myself saying these things from the outside, and what I wanted to do in that instant, after observing myself, was shoot myself, right in the head. I'd had two drinks, three max, and already I couldn't believe it was me talking.

I got up, then, to move around the room a little, to see if I could find where I'd put the ice bucket. When I sat down again, Paul asked if I was married. Married? It stopped me for a moment—the question did. Apparently, he thought I would get married and not invite him to my wedding—not even tell him about it. Which meant that now, when I did get married, I basically *couldn't* invite him, even if I wanted to. Then I asked if *he* was married, half joking, and he said no, but he was engaged. I practically jumped through the phone when he told me that. I told him I couldn't believe he hadn't told me. But he didn't respond to that; he just said it was to a girl I didn't know—a girl named Christine. But I did know her, I said. Or at least I'd met her. They'd started dating right before I left for Toledo. Where? Paul said—where did I meet her? At Sevens, I said, remember? Sevens was the kind of place

that made you want to run straight down to the Golden Gate Bridge and jump, but for a long time I was going there every night of the week. Paul said he remembered now.

We talked for a few more minutes, and finally I told him I was actually in San Francisco at that very moment. I hadn't decided if I was going to mention it or not, but I did, and he said he couldn't believe it. You should come over to our place for dinner, he said. When? I said. Right now, he said. Right now? I said. And he said, Sure, why not? But then before I could even really say anything else, he told me to hold on—he said he had to double-check with Christine. And he put me on hold, on actual hold, as if I was talking to the gas company. There was a time, I have to say, when Paul never double-checked anything with anyone. But now—I was on hold for a quite a long time, too.

I knew what they were talking about: Christine didn't like me. It was obvious the night we met. For starters, she's about five inches taller than I am, and we were at Sevens, where it's always very very loud, and she kept having to bend down to hear what I had to say. And even then I had to shout basically directly into her ear. I was probably spitting all over the side of her head. She was annoyed by the whole situation, I could tell, and she cut things off pretty quickly. The whole conversation lasted about forty-five seconds, and then she went back to sipping her martini and swishing her tongue around the inside of Paul's ear.

Four days later, I was a resident of Toledo, Ohio. When you start hanging out with people like that, you know it's time to pack up and leave town. Otherwise, you just end up killing yourself when you turn forty.

Finally Paul came back on the line. First he asked if I was still there. I said I was—where would I have gone? Then he said I was welcome to come over. But the way he said it—somehow, now it felt as if I'd invited myself over. I told him I didn't have to come, but he said it was fine; if he didn't want me to come, he wouldn't have invited me. Then, after a second, he said I should stop on the way and pick up some food for myself, anything I might want to eat. Christine had already made dinner, he said, and she'd only made enough for two, since she wasn't expecting me at the time—he admitted

that it sounded strange, to invite someone over for dinner and then tell them to pick something up on the way. I was fine with it, though, and I told him so, but what was I supposed to pick up? I asked him that—I asked him that directly. I said, Like beef? Pork? What? Whatever I felt like, he said. Like pizza? Like a hamburger? He said it didn't matter, except that it shouldn't be anything that required cooking, since Christine was done cooking for the night. That's fine, I said. I wasn't expecting anyone to cook for me. I said I understood, and then I asked for his address.

And then what I did was, I didn't pick anything up. I just didn't feel like it. I wasn't even hungry, and besides I thought I might just puke it up again when Christine started to say anything.

When I got there, though, it seemed like Paul wasn't going to notice—we hadn't seen each other in about a thousand years, after all. The first thing he said was "Roger!" And then he opened his arms and we hugged—this was right in the doorway, too, practically on the street. All kinds of people could have seen us as they walked by.

"Lansker!" I said. "Lansk-doggier!" Which is what we used to call him back in college. And then I gave him this gigantic bear hug that lifted him completely from the ground for a moment, which is something I like to do from time to time, even though I'm only about five-foot-seven. It's a nervous reaction, to be perfectly honest. I can't help myself.

After I put him down, he waved me inside, still smiling, and said it was extremely good to see me, which is exactly what I said to him in return, and then he said I looked great, which was a lie. I looked like hell—I wasn't healthy at all. In fact, I'd recently been *losing* weight, and I'd developed these hard purple welts around my neck. Paul genuinely did look great, though; it looked like he'd been taking vitamins and lifting weights.

Then he said, "Where's your food?"

I told him I decided not to stop. "Don't worry, I'm not hungry," I said. "I'll just drink a lot."

He looked a little annoyed. "That's what I'm afraid of," he said.

And I paused for a moment when he said

that. What an interesting comment, I thought. Because the thing was, I couldn't tell if he was serious or not. He didn't laugh or anything afterward. I was going to ask what he meant by that, exactly, but then Christine appeared at the top of the stairs— we were still on our way up—wearing a kitchen apron over some professional-looking outfit. I realized then, for the first time, that I had almost no recollection of her face from the night I'd met her.

"Hello!" I said—I practically shouted it, actually. I was already a little drunk, quite honestly, but not bad, not bad at all. Paul said he'd forgotten that Christine and I had met, which I already knew, because he'd said the same thing on the phone, and Christine confirmed that we'd met at Sevens. Then I admitted that I hadn't brought any food, because I could see she was a little annoyed, but at Paul, not at me. She was assuming Paul had forgotten to tell me to pick something up and that now I was expecting dinner. I clarified the situation, though. I told her Paul had asked me to pick something up but that I'd decided not to because I wasn't hungry. It wasn't true, of course—I was practically starving.

"Are you sure?" she said. She was just being polite.

"Absolutely," I said. "I've been eating all day."

Christine returned to the kitchen to finish dinner, and Paul started to show me around the place. It was obviously a very fancy place—very high end, all of it. It felt like you were standing in a magazine spread. Christine's father was probably paying for it. We were standing in the living room, and Paul wanted to give me a full tour, to show me all the features, but I wasn't paying any attention—I was busy looking for something. For his birthday I once gave Paul a very expensive and classy orna-mental glass bowl, and I wanted to see if he still had it. I was just curious; for some reason, I'd been thinking about it on the way over. So while he was talking, I was walking around the room and looking over all the shelves and tables; I even opened a few drawers. I may have been breathing sort of heavily. I was sweating, I know that; I'd been sweating for about an hour straight.

Paul, though, he knew exactly what I was looking for. "It's on the mantel," he said.

He was right. It was sitting right there on the corner, overlooking the entire room—a prominent position. The light was shining

through it. It was just a little too close to the edge, though, so I pushed it back gently with the tip of my finger.

"Would you like some wine?" Paul asked.

"Yes!" I said. "Yes, I would."

He took a glass from the cabinet—two were already set on the table—filled it halfway, and handed it to me. Then he filled his completely, and I think he was about to propose a toast, but Christine came in again from the kitchen. She was holding two dinner plates, which she put on the table, and she asked Paul to light the candles and get the chicken from the oven. I almost went with him, but when Christine sat down, she invited me to join her. I didn't want to— I can't stand it when this sort of thing happens. I mean I really hate it. I couldn't think of anything to say—not a word. Not even a sound. I was just staring at the inseam of my pants.

"Do you like Toledo?" she asked after a minute. She was folding her napkin across her lap.

It was a terrible thing to ask—a depressing thing to ask. But I said something—I must have said something. I think I said something about the low housing prices and the quality of the drinking water. It was some place in Oregon I was describing, actually; I'd read about it on the plane on the way out. But I didn't know what else to say.

"It's hot in the summer, isn't it?" she asked.

"Quite," I said, "but I live right along the river." Then I said something about the river that made it out to be really scenic and beautiful.

She said that sounded nice—living along the river.

I said it was pretty nice. "Do you guys still go to Sevens?" I asked.

She shook her head. "Doesn't Sevens stop letting you in the door when you turn thirty?"

I said I hadn't heard that. I said, "Personally, I hate Sevens."

She looked surprised. "You used to go there all the time, didn't you?"

"Every single night," I said. "But I always hated it." She nodded vaguely, and I didn't know if she understood me or not. By now

I was conducting the entire conversation with my head basically inside my wine glass.

"Have you found any good places in Toledo?" she asked.

"The Black Bar," I said. "If you and Paul ever come visit, I'll take you there."

Paul came back into the room then. He had their chicken split up on a big dish, and he put half of it on Christine's plate. Then he sat down, put his napkin in his lap, picked up his wine glass, and proposed a toast. "To Roger," he said, "for coming back to visit us after all these years."

We drank, and they started to eat, and I reached for the wine bottle. For a minute, there was complete silence. They seemed hungry. They ate, and I watched them eat, and then for some reason I closed my eyes and *listened* to them eat, and as I did this, as I listened to them eat, I had this sudden desire to go back to Toledo— to just get up from the table and leave, right at that very moment, without even saying anything or explaining why I was leaving. I should have never called him, I said to myself. It was a horrible mistake. But right then, at the moment when I most wanted to leave, I was also remembering that Chaney was angry at me, and that I hadn't even seen him in over a month. I'd essentially had to stop going to the Black Bar altogether. It had started there, of course, just down the street from my apartment. Chaney had been talking to this woman for hours, which was nothing new. All he wanted to do was get laid. He was like an animal. He came over to me around midnight and asked for the keys to my apartment, and I gave them to him without even really thinking about it; I'd had about ten beers, and I was busy watching a football game. I wasn't paying attention. But eventually closing time came, and Chaney still hadn't come back with my keys, and I started to get a little annoyed—my car was outside, and I didn't want to leave it there overnight. I didn't even know if Chaney was still at my place, or if he'd gone somewhere else and just forgotten about my keys, or what. So I walked home, and when I got there, Chaney's car was in front, parked diagonally in the carport. I walked upstairs and knocked, but there was no answer. I knocked again, and there was still no answer. So I knocked again, and then again, and then I just kept knocking. I probably knocked for about forty-five minutes straight.

I knocked until Chaney finally opened the door—until he threw it open, as a matter of fact. He was standing there in a full sweat, buck naked except for a condom, and before I could even say anything he called me a baby, a little baby, which I found to be an interesting choice of words, and then he said that if he wasn't in the middle of fucking the living shit out of this woman, he would beat me to a tiny pulp right there on the spot. And that was it. After that, he turned and walked back into the bedroom.

I stood there for a second, and then I went inside and sat on the couch in the living room. I didn't want to turn on the television too loud, because it might make Chaney even angrier, so what I did was, I turned it on at a very low volume and sat down right in front of it, in the dark, just a few inches away. It's weird—when you watch television like that, your eyes burn like hell for about a minute, but then something happens, and they stop hurting, and everything just goes white.

When I got up later to go to the bathroom, I realized that the reason I could hear them so clearly was that Chaney hadn't even bothered to close the door. I didn't mean to see them—I didn't *want* to see them—but the bedroom was on the way to the bathroom, and the door was open, and I couldn't close the door because it opened in. I ended up staying there for a minute to watch them anyway, because—I don't even know why, but not for the reason you might think. For one thing, Chaney was standing on the bed, still naked, obviously, and he was holding a belt. He looked like he was going to hit her with it. After that I tried to go outside to the balcony for a while, but the lizard fish was down there in the mud and leaves, and I thought I could actually *hear* him slithering around. I couldn't bear it.

When Chaney finally left I was just sitting there in the dark again, wide awake. He came into the living room with the girl hanging on his shoulder and threw my keys at me. He said, "Here you go, baby." And when the girl laughed, he said it again. He said, "See you later, baby." And she laughed a little more.

I'd only seen Chaney one time after that. It was at the Black Bar, but he pretended I wasn't there, and when I pushed him on the shoulder, he pushed me back in a different way, and I left.

* * *

I said to Paul, then, while I was thinking about this, I said, "Do you remember freshman year when we got drunk and stole the piano from the student center?"

He looked up from his chicken. It took him a moment, but he said of course he remembered.

"Do you think that was our greatest prank?" I asked him.

He thought about that, too, and then he said he couldn't remember any other pranks.

I nearly leapt out of my seat. "What about the streetlights? Or the bell? Or the rabbits?"

He smiled, then—he remembered now. I watched him closely: it was all coming back to him. Then he said, "The piano was better. How could you beat the piano?"

"You couldn't beat the piano!" I said. "Nobody could figure out how we got it out of the building!" It was thrilling to think about even now. I was sort of hopping around in my chair. Then I asked him, "What was your single favorite moment?"

"Of what?" he asked.

"Of college!" I said. "What's the one memory that keeps coming back to you? If you had to pick one."

"Of all of college?" he said.

"Sure. Or of freshman year. Whatever. What sticks in your mind the most?"

But he still looked a little confused. "You mean—?"

"The moment that first comes to mind," I said, impatiently. "The one that first pops up when you think about that time." I was leaning over the table now—I was practically on *top* of the table now.

"I guess I don't know," he said. "Maybe arriving on the first day and not knowing anyone."

"You knew Hoff," I reminded him. They'd gone to prep school together.

"That's true," he said. "But I didn't know you or Gill or Burke."

"Still, you knew Hoff. That doesn't count. Think of another one."

He tried, briefly, but then he said, "I think that's it, Roger. That's the one that comes to mind."

I found it rather unbelievable that that's

what Paul remembered most from freshman year. I could think of a thousand things that were more memorable than that.

"What about you?" Christine asked suddenly, almost out of nowhere.

There was one night, I remember, when we were coming back from a bar maybe twenty or thirty minutes from campus, and there wasn't enough room in the car for everyone. We'd arrived in two cars, but one of them had left early, so Paul and I agreed to ride in the trunk on the way home. It was an actual trunk, too—the trunk of a sedan. It wasn't very big, either, and it was completely full of crap, so what we did was, as soon as we pulled onto the highway, we started throwing everything out—beach chairs, cassettes, hats, umbrellas, golf clubs, bottles of water, tennis rackets, shoes, towels, jumper cables, flashlights. It didn't matter—we threw it all out. It wasn't even this kid's car, either. It was his *father's* car—his father's stuff. He'd just borrowed it for the weekend. But we didn't care. We chucked everything onto the highway, into the night, and watched it crack up and disintegrate in the darkness. For a while, we were just sitting with our feet hanging out the back, passing a plastic bottle of vodka back and forth and looking up at the night, but then we thought we saw a cop, and we crowded inside and pulled the top down. I don't know why, but without saying as much, we both seemed to feel that we were right then experiencing the greatest moment of our lives. At one point we clasped hands in the total blackness of that trunk and swore to remain best friends forever. It was the kind of thing you do when you're twelve years old, but we were eighteen, and we were far from home, and we were in the trunk of a car going eighty miles an hour down a New Jersey highway at four o'clock in the morning.

I didn't say any of that to Paul and Christine, though. I just said, "The thing about the piano was that Gill and Hoff and Burke weren't even involved—they weren't even *there* for it."

"That's true," said Paul, thinking back. "I'd forgotten about that."

"It was just the two of us," I said. I glanced over at Christine when I said it. For some reason, I had the sense that she was passing judgment on everything I said. "Did you ever notice that about them?" I asked.

"What?" he said.

"That they disappear at all the key moments—that they're never there when it really counts."

"I don't know," he said. "What do you mean 'key moments'?"

"Key moments," I said. "Important, memorable moments. They always miss them."

Paul said he'd never noticed it.

"But do you notice it now that I mention it?"

Paul tried to think back. "Give me an example," he said.

"The piano," I said, "for one."

"Right," he said. "Okay." He didn't seem convinced.

I looked over at Christine again, and then back at Paul. "What about the trunk of Stern's car on the way back from Frank's Chicken Shack?"

It took a moment for Paul to remember what I was talking about—to bring it to mind.

"What happened in the trunk of Stern's car on the way back from Frank's Chicken Shack?" asked Christine.

But Paul ignored her. He was back in New Jersey, I could tell, on the highway, in the trunk, with me. Then he answered my question: "They were *inside* the car."

"My point exactly," I said.

"What's your point exactly?"

But all of a sudden I didn't feel like going into it anymore. "Forget it," I said. "Let's talk about something else."

I looked over at Christine. "So where's the wedding?" I said to her. But before she even had a chance to answer, I turned back to Paul and said, "You know, Paul, out of our group of friends, even from the beginning, you were the only one I ever really respected—the only one I ever really *liked*. Gill, Hoff, Burke—I mean, they're—"

But I stopped, then, I didn't continue, because I could see that Paul was annoyed by what I was saying. He'd put down his knife and fork and stiffened in his chair. I believe he even sighed.

"What?" I said. "What's wrong? Why did you sigh?"

"I'm sorry, but I just don't feel like having this conversation again," he said.

"What do you mean *again*?" I said. I admit,

I was getting a little frustrated. My voice was getting louder.

"We've been over this before," he said.

I said, "I don't know why it bothers you so much. It's actually a compliment to you. I'm saying—"

"I know what you're saying," he said.

"Then why don't you want to talk about it?"

"Because Gill and Hoff and Burke are still friends of mine, close friends of mine, and if you decided for some reason, at some point, that you didn't like them, that's fine, but it makes me uncomfortable to talk about it."

"I *never* liked them," I clarified. "I didn't decide at some point that I didn't like them—I *never* liked them."

"We were together every day for four years in college!" he said. "And we lived together in the city after that!"

"I never liked them," I said again. "In fact, I hated them. I hated them from the first minute."

"I just don't understand how that can be," said Paul.

"And frankly," I said, "I don't recall that we've ever talked about this before."

And at that, he looked at me in disbelief. He said, "Sevens?"

"What about Sevens?"

"The last night you were here," he said. "The last night we even saw you!"

Of course, I knew then exactly what he was talking about. Very quickly, it became perfectly clear in my mind. Everyone was there. Gill, Hoff, Burke, Paul, me, Gill's girlfriend, Hoff's girlfriend, Christine, maybe a few others—basically everyone, everyone I knew in the entire world. The thing was, that night, of all the nights we'd ended up there, we had managed to get these seats at the back of the bar— the kind of seats you get maybe once in a lifetime at Sevens. Usually you wore yourself out standing. Everyone stood—you didn't have a choice. But in the back there were these luxurious, overstuffed couches and armchairs, set up around a heavy oak coffee table. I didn't even know what you had to do to get these seats, because I had never seen them open. There were always people sitting there when I arrived. But that night I got there first out of our

group, which I always do, because I'm an extremely punctual person, and I ordered three beers so I didn't have to return to the bar right away. I wasn't even planning on walking back there to look, because I figured it was a waste of time, but then I caught a glimpse through the crowd and saw that nobody was sitting there. Right away I ran over and spread everything out. I draped my jacket over the chair and distributed my beers to the far corners of the table; I lay down across the couch. Other people tried to sit down, but I told them absolutely not. I told them a pretty big party was coming, and the entire thing was saved. I could hardly wait for my friends. How impressed were they going to be? How speechless? How grateful?

A few hours later, the table was covered with martini glasses and beer bottles, and the candlelight through the glass was making everything look sparkly and happy and beautiful. We were all there, all of our friends, and the best part was that I had the most important chair, the overstuffed tan one with the ottoman, right at the head of the table. It was even slightly taller than the other chairs and couches, so that I was looking down on everything, just sort of presiding. I wasn't even really talking to anyone. I was just watching and listening. But the thing was, I had to go to the bathroom—I had to go to the bathroom terribly. I'd been drinking practically all day and it was starting to catch up with me. I tried to hold it—but I'd already been holding it for hours. I even thought about just going right there in my pants. I'd done it before—in a bar like Sevens, where everything's dark, and where every-one's busy talking, nobody ever notices. And then I wouldn't have to get up. But what I did instead was, I leaned over and asked Hoff, who was sitting on the couch next to my chair, to guard my seat. He said he would, and then I spread my jacket across the chair, from one end to the other, to signal that it was saved.

In the bathroom, standing there at the urinal, alone, I leaned back and closed my eyes and turned my face to the ceiling. I felt suddenly good about things, and I reminded myself not to forget it, because it doesn't often happen like this—you don't always get those chairs, and you don't always have everyone there, and you don't always drink just the perfect amount.

But when I returned, my jacket was on the floor and Gill was sitting in the chair. I went up to Hoff first—discreetly, because I didn't

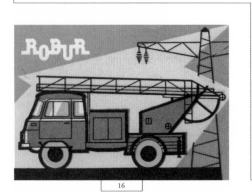

want to make a scene—and said I thought I asked him to guard my seat, but he brushed me off and told me to talk to Gill, since he was the one sitting there. So I leaned over and politely explained to Gill that I had been saving the seat while I went to the bathroom and that I was back from the bathroom now and was ready to sit down again. But he said he didn't want to move. I said I had gotten there first out of everyone tonight and saved all the seats and that the least he could do was let me have this one. But he shook his head and said he didn't care. I said I had always wanted to sit in this seat—I said it was my favorite seat in the entire bar, if not the entire world, and that I had never gotten to sit in it before tonight, never in my life, and that I would really appreciate it if he would let me sit in it just this one time. He said if I went and bought him a beer, he would give me the seat back. So I did. I went and bought him a beer, but when I gave it to him, he still wouldn't move. I asked him again to let me have the seat, but by now he was completely ignoring me—pretending that I wasn't even there. So I kept asking him, a little louder each time. I asked him four or five times, practically talking right into his ear, because I wanted to make sure he heard me. He ignored me every time. Then he leaned over and started talking to this girl—this girl who I had never even *seen* before, this girl who wasn't even part of our group. There were no other seats, either. I was the only one standing—everyone else was sitting. I felt like such an idiot—I hate standing when everyone else is sitting. I couldn't hear anything that was being said. From where I stood, everything was just a loud, hollow murmur, a dead murmur, just noise around my head. So what I did was, I started to say a few things myself, even though I had no idea what they were all talking about; I thought, if I proposed a topic, I might be able to get back into the conversation. I just threw a few things out there. For instance, I said something about my little brother who when he was four reached up and turned the knob on the front door and walked out into the street. And then I stopped—I didn't continue, because I wanted to see if anyone was paying attention. Someone said so what happened, and I said a car ran over him and crushed his chest and skull in and he died. And then someone said something in response to I don't know what and the entire table erupted into laughter. I said, What? I said,

What's so funny? But nobody answered. So I leaned over and asked Gill what was so funny, and he said, Oh, nothing. And so what I started to do then was talk at great volume, at ever increasing volume, and what I talked about was what Paul had just referred to—I started to talk about Gill and Hoff and Burke and what incredible assholes they were and how I had always hated them and how Gill had fucked Hoff's girlfriend twice, which was true—it was just one night, but twice that night—and which Hoff didn't even *know*, all of which finally got everyone's attention and made everyone go real quiet, which was when Paul grabbed me by the collar and dragged me over to the corner of the bar and told me I was drunk and an embarrassment and what was my problem and that if I wanted to have any friends left in the morning, if it wasn't already too late, I should go home right now and sleep it off. I told him I didn't care about any of them, about whether they were my friends or not. I told him I'd never liked them, and that he was the only one I ever really respected, the only one I ever really liked.

I can't remember exactly what happened after that. I left—I know that—and I left without my jacket, because I remember nearly freezing to death down by the Presidio, near the water, a few hours later. It was one of those nights where you sort of instinctively, without even really knowing it, make your way across the city toward the Golden Gate Bridge—where one moment you're drinking in a bar on Russian Hill and the next you've lost your coat and you're in the fog on Greenwich crossing Broderick and the cars are flying by about an inch away on either side and you can smell the salt and the eucalyptus and see the heavy angel wings of the bridge all lit up and shining. Except that night I didn't make it that far. I ended up talking to some guy who was just standing there on the corner of Greenwich and Van Ness. I remember we talked for about three hours—and I remember that because we were basically standing *inside* a fog bank, and it was cold as hell, and I remember shivering like I'd never shivered before. It was like a seizure—my whole body was shaking. I remember I told him all about what had just happened and that he said they probably didn't mean anything by it, and I remember laughing when he said that. I remember laughing and laughing and laughing and laughing and laughing—laughing the

way only a drunk person laughs. I remember telling him about Paul. I remember telling him about the car ride with Paul that I told you about already. I remember telling him about my little brother. I remember saying that there was no place more beautiful than the Golden Gate Bridge at night. And after I told him that, I remember saying that I had to go and starting down the sidewalk toward the bridge, and then I remember him tugging on the sleeve of my shirt and saying the bridge would be there any old night.

So that's what Paul was referring to, when he said we'd talked about it before, though I'm not even sure whether that counts or not. Anyway, I did an embarrassing thing then. A stupid thing. I did something I shouldn't have done. I did something that I hated—that I hated myself for doing. This is why I always want to kill myself—just so I won't do these things again. It's the only sure way.

Paul had gone back to eating; we were calming down. He was really going at it, too, cutting his chicken up like crazy and spearing it with his fork and shoving it into his mouth. I drank some more wine, silently, and then for some reason I wanted him to stop, to put his fork and knife down and just stop eating for a minute so we could start talking again. I said something, but he didn't hear me, and then I said something again. Maybe I said it too quietly, I don't know, but when he still didn't respond, I reached across the table with my dirty claw and grabbed a whole fistful of rice directly from Paul's plate and stuffed it in my mouth, all at once, my entire fist, or as much of it as I could. I couldn't fit everything in—my fist was too big—and rice was spilling out all over the place, but I tried to jam it in, even then, and when I pulled my fist out, there was blood on my hand, from my knuckles cutting against my teeth.

"*Jesus*," Paul said. He pushed his chair back and jumped up, as if I might go after him next.

I couldn't talk. I could hardly breathe. Paul was furious. He was disgusted. He said, "What the *fuck*, Roger?"

I didn't even look at Christine. I couldn't. I just put my head down and tried to swallow the rice as quickly as possible.

LEONA PAEGLES

When I could speak again, when I'd swallowed it all, I was practically crying. Not much, not much at all, but a little. I said I was sorry. I said I shouldn't have done that. "I'm sorry, Paul," I said. I said it about a hundred times.

"You're drunk," Paul said.

"I'm not drunk," I said, shaking my head.

"Yes, you are," he said. "I smelled it on your breath when you got here."

"I'm not drunk," I said again. "I'm hungry."

"I told you to bring something," he said.

"I didn't want to bring anything," I told him.

By now Christine had picked up her plate and gone back to the kitchen. I didn't know what she was doing—I thought maybe she was going to call the cops.

"You could have given me some of yours," I was saying. "You had enough."

"But I *told* you to bring something," Paul said. He was yelling now. He was pretty angry at me.

Christine came back in, then. She was carrying a plate of food in one hand and something else—something I couldn't make out—in the other. She came around to my side of the table.

"Here, Roger," she said, and put the plate down in front of me. She'd put her dinner on a fresh plate, and she'd cut off the part of the chicken that she'd been eating. It looked brand new. She said she wasn't hungry anyway, that I could have it. Then she sat down next to me and took my hand—the hand that was bleeding—in her own. "Eat," she told me.

And while I ate, awkwardly, with my left hand, she rolled up my sleeve and started to clean the cuts with a damp cloth, making these patient, tender little dabs with it across my knuckles. It stung, but not too bad. She was so careful—so slow. And the other thing was, while she was doing this, she was sort of rubbing me on the back with her other hand—just very lightly, right in the middle, in a circular motion, just these gentle, soft little rubs. It confused me for a moment—I was even going to ask her to stop, but I couldn't. I mean I really couldn't.

The amazing thing—the most amazing thing of all—was that, after that, we actually had a pretty nice evening. Christine cleared

the table when we were done, and then she stayed in the kitchen and did all the dishes, which gave Paul and me a chance to talk for a while. We talked about a lot of things, too. I told him I couldn't believe that he'd never called me—never even bothered to see if I was still alive or not—and he reminded me that he *had* called me. He'd called my mother to get my number and left a whole series of messages, but I had just never called him back—which was true, and which I'd forgotten about. Even Burke had called me, he reminded me. And that was true, too. We talked just like this—just sort of going over everything and reminding ourselves of things and remembering different times. Paul opened another bottle of wine and offered me some, but I didn't have too much more. At one point, Christine even brought in two huge bowls of chocolate ice cream for us.

After a while, when it was time for me to go, I gave Christine a big hug, not a big bear hug, but a generous hug nevertheless, and said goodbye, and then Paul walked me down the stairs and opened the door for me. I stepped out onto the sidewalk and looked up and down the street. The fog was everywhere—you could barely even see the streetlights.

For some reason, then, standing there, looking around at the fog and the dark apartment buildings, I told Paul my mom had just died—just a few weeks ago, in fact. It was a lie—my mom was living happily in Fort Lauderdale with her second husband—but I said it anyway.

Paul said he was sorry.

I said she'd died after a long and painful bout with liver cancer.

Paul said he was sorry again.

I told him that he was always her favorite—that of all my friends, she'd liked him the best. Which was true, actually—that part. And I said she had mentioned his name on her deathbed.

"Really?" he asked.

I nodded. "She said she hoped we would stay friends."

Neither one of us said anything for a moment about that. We looked up and down the street and squinted through the dense fog.

Then Paul said, "Let's do that. Let's do what she said. Let's stay friends."

I smiled. "All right," I said.

We shook hands—Paul standing in the doorway, me on the sidewalk.

"You know what you should do?" I said to him.

"What's that?" he said.

"You should invite me to your wedding. I'd like to be there. I'd like to be there as you start your new life with Christine."

And he said he would do that—he said he would like to have me there.

We said goodbye one last time, and then he closed the door.

I turned and started to walk down the street, but I stopped before I reached the end of the block, and what I did was, I found a piece of loose concrete on the curb—it was just sitting there, as if I had been meant to find it, a five- or ten-pound piece that had come free somehow, a big, heavy, jagged piece. I picked it up, and with two hands, sort of over my shoulder, because it was so heavy, I heaved it into the air and through Paul's bay window, directly into his living room.

Man, was that a loud noise! I was standing right below the window—glass rained down all over me! I heard a scream inside, too—it was Christine, and I wondered if I'd hit her, if she'd been sitting on the couch by the window or something—but, I don't know, all of it was in the far distance by then anyway. I was already gone. I was running down the street, running as fast as I could, running like I was a little kid again, just running and running and running. I ran practically across the entire goddamn city—I mean, out of Cole Valley, through the Haight, nearly right past the apartment where Paul and Gill and Hoff and Burke and I used to live, past the field where I would sit sometimes and watch Little League games, where on Saturdays there would be about a thousand dogs, where from the top you can see the ocean and the freighters coming in, although tonight it all just looked like darkness, like empty space, and down, down those steep, long stairs, taking them four or five at a time, through the backyards of the wealthy people, to the Marina—all the way until I could smell the salt water. It took me about an hour, running the whole time. It was a pretty long way. My plan was to keep running, too, all the way to the bridge, but for some reason I stopped as I crossed Baker, because I saw a

pay phone right there, and what I did was, I called up Chaney back in Ohio. It was probably three o'clock in the morning for him, but he answered anyway. I knew he would.

I said, "Chaney! It's Roger!"

He didn't respond right away—there was a fairly long silence. Frankly, I'm not sure what he was thinking about. I hadn't talked to him in a month.

Then he said, "Where are you?"

I could tell now that he was excited to hear from me; I could tell from his voice, not necessarily from what he said. He may have still been a little mad, but he was excited to hear from me nevertheless.

I told him I was in San Francisco.

"What are you doing there?" he wanted to know.

I told him I was out here on business.

He said I sounded drunk.

I said I was dead sober, and then I said, "Listen, Chaney, I just wanted to let you know that I'm coming home."

"What?" he said.

I was on a pay phone—the connection was terrible. I said, "I'm coming home! Back to Toledo, tomorrow morning, first thing!"

"Did you call me at three o'clock in the morning just to tell me that?"

"Yes," I said, "I did." Who knows what he was thinking about at this point? He didn't say anything for about a minute—nothing.

But then he said, "Well, call me when you get back into town."

And I said I would—I said I would do that. I said I would call him tomorrow afternoon, as soon as I got into town.

And he said fine.

And I said maybe we could go out for a beer.

And he said sure.

And I said, on me—the beers would be on me.

And he said that sounded good.

And that was it. We hung up. I started walking back to my hotel—I was too tired to run now. I walked all the way back downtown. And when I got there, to my room,

I didn't even go to sleep—I just stood in the shower for about an hour and a half, and then I watched television until the sun came up and the fog burned off and it was time to go to the airport, and that was the last time I ever went to San Francisco or saw my old friend Paul.

neaizmirstiet

The Strauss House

DAWN RYAN

ÚZV 68

**POHYBEM
PROTI OTYLOSTI**

Solo Lipník · ČSN 49 4705

Barbara and Sam met their freshman year in high school running cross country on the JV team. Barbara had always been an athlete, but Sam hadn't. She was one of those girls who had a lot of muscle but didn't know what to do with it, and she had joined the team partly because she'd recently diagnosed herself with a mild form of Tourette's after watching a *Dateline* special. A girl they'd profiled had found that distance running helped allay her symptoms. Sam had a tendency to do that, to try on obscure neurological ailments, see which fit, and then see if she could cure them. She ended up being one of the fastest on the team, which wasn't saying much, but Barbara was faster than she was. The only time Sam beat her was when Barbara tripped and sprained her ankle. The chivalric thing to do would have been to stop and help her, but Barbara urged Sam to keep going, hoping that one of them might actually outrun one of their opponents for the first time in Belmont junior varsity history. Sam ran so fast she pissed her pants a little. Barbara was the only one who noticed, who knew it wasn't sweat; and the piss, for whatever reason, made Barbara proud.

Barbara and her brother, Steven, were adopted. They were black and their parents were white, a distinction Mr. and Mrs. Strauss had hoped their money would make irrelevant. But they couldn't avoid the minor racial indignities, the micro-aggressions, one being this assumption about money making us colorblind, which caused Barbara to feel like her race was a costume. It was confusing for Barbara, and she couldn't wait to tell Sam all about it, because even though Sam was white, and Sam's parents were white, Barbara knew Sam had a weird family too, and maybe Sam would understand, if Barbara could just get her to come home with her. Barbara had been trying for some time. There was a joke she wanted to tell Sam, too, a family joke about how when the adoption agency had inquired about racial preferences, the Strausses had muted whatever inclinations they had toward little white babies and claimed no preference at all, and how, in an act of obvious reaction-formation, however benign, Mrs. Strauss began boasting that *If we're adopting, we're adopting black.* This became an ongoing family punch line, resurrected twice for the rescue of shelter kittens and a third time for the purchase of a purebred Belgian shepherd. Barbara didn't like this joke so much. Barbara had better jokes, funnier jokes. She had one about how she didn't discover she was black until she was in kindergarten, didn't know she was different from her parents. How she had a mini-breakdown, went a little mad, but now she couldn't be more grateful, knowing who she wasn't. Barbara never told anybody that one.

The Strausses lived in a big Victorian house at the top of a hill. Mr. Strauss had supposedly been writing his Ph.D. dissertation for the past fifteen years. He had a restless mind and couldn't stick to a thesis. The house was evidence of this. When Barbara finally got Sam to come home with her she gave Sam a tour of her father's office, pointing out different things within the twisted miscellany. The walls were covered with creepy dioramas of taxidermied animals performing mundane middle-class scenes: watching TV, reading the newspaper, playing golf. He had a squirrel in a doctor's coat standing over another squirrel in stirrups, for a pap. Just below it, on the mantel, was a family photo.

Barbara stared at Sam staring at the squirrels. She was getting ideas.

"Me and Steven used to play doctor," Barbara said, "like the squirrels. We had to be shamed out of it."

"That's sort of sick," Sam said.

Barbara shrugged. "It happens. If you want it to, it could happen."

Barbara was being coy, but Sam didn't know what this meant. She wasn't ready to figure it out.

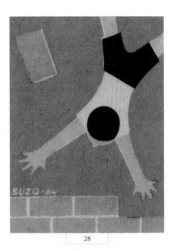

The house had a servant's quarters, which the Strausses kept as a spare bedroom. This is where Sam stayed when she'd all but moved in, when Barbara had all but forced her to move in. She slept over so often Mr. and Mrs. Strauss began referring to their attic apartment as the Trombone Suite. Sam's last name was Trombone. Sam's mom, Mrs. Trombone, was so high she had amnesia. Most of the time she forgot about her daughter altogether, and when she remembered she didn't care. The Strausses cared too much, wanted her there all the time. At least Barbara did, and Mr. Strauss did too. He was a collector of odd things, and Sam was an odd thing. There was something boyish about her, something gender-bending that hadn't gotten to the point of severity, and Mr. Strauss had just begun writing about the Egyptian hermaphrodite. His interest didn't pass by Barbara, who wasn't sure if she liked it or not, this potential rivalry for her friend's affection, or for her father's.

"Ever think of cutting your hair, Samuel?" Mr. Strauss asked her one afternoon. "Or wearing hats?"

The girls had just gotten back from track practice, and Sam was looking especially brawny.

"Leave her alone, Dad," Barbara said.

"It's just a suggestion," Mr. Strauss said. "Maybe a fedora, or a pillbox. Something classy."

"Leave her alone, Dad," Barbara said.

"Why, you're both so strange and cute, I just want to bash your heads together, mix your faces all up," Mr. Strauss said, squishing his own face into a distorted mess. His skin was like putty.

Barbara gave him a little kick in the leg, said, "Leave us alone, Dad." And that was that.

"I know, he's fucking crazy," Barbara said, after her father had left the room. "Every time he changes his thesis he goes a little more nuts. We've decided."

"I don't mind," Sam told her. "It's better than nothing at all."

Sam loved the servant's quarters, the Trombone Suite, loved sleeping under their servant quilts, reading the collection of *Architectural Digest*s for servants. And she loved flossing. Servant's flossing was a new practice she'd picked up in the servant apartment, to ward off servant tooth decay and the mind rot she'd read about in the Russian novels strewn along the servant walls. She loved whatever else she did up there, alone, sometimes not alone. And Sam liked waking up in that house, having breakfast every morning with her choice of maple syrup from the kitchen cupboard that housed only maple syrups, over a dozen to choose from, and so much butter! She'd learned that butter was meant to be left unsalted and unrefrigerated or why bother, unless you're getting

the government stuff and you don't really have a choice, she'd inform them, which made them feel even more sophisticated, more worldly, knowing a person who got the government stuff.

Sam never wanted to leave. It was so much better than being alone, so much better than biding time waiting for the next nervous tic. Before long Sam had entered the family routine: breakfast in the morning, then off to school, track practice in the afternoon, then homework, dinner, TV, and bed. What was so normal and boring to Barbara felt wonderfully rich and exotic to Sam. It was like this with their history class, a class Sam had begged and pleaded to take and a class Barbara had begged and pleaded not to take. The Strausses were both on the school committee and had demanded that Barbara enroll in every advanced class offered. Sam had taken to caring about herself, a care that manifested itself in intellectual diligence, thorough dental hygiene, and constant dread of mental break. She was certain it would happen, if it hadn't already. They were supposed to be reading the *Rights of Man*, and Sam was determined to appear studious for fear they'd send her to the classrooms in the basement, with the other kids from her part of town. The rumors were that people did crazy things down there. Sam did not want to do crazy things. Her nervousness was a nervousness that looked conventional. It looked like shyness. Barbara always wanted to talk, though.

"I wish my dad was a badass like yours," she said to Sam in class one day.

"My father's not a badass, he's an idiot," Sam whispered. Bobby Trombone, one of the town winos, had already gone mad. He lived with Sam's grandmother in a Section 8 apartment and spent most of his nights riding his ten-speed to the VFW, where he drank and blew lines of coke in the bathroom. He was a disabled vet and Sam hardly knew him. He'd eventually get hit by a car, she was sure, riding his bike along the Newton side of the Charles River. There was a dangerous stretch of two-way traffic where people drove too fast, and Bobby Trombone would be smashed by an old man in a purple Sonata coming off the Mass Pike. The old man would swerve, fishtail, and send Bobby flying into the water. It wouldn't kill him, in fact he'd get a nice settlement from the insurance company which might help Sam with college tuition, but

eventually he'd become addicted to the oxy scrip the doctors would give him for the pain, and that's how he'd die. Sam was certain of it.

Barbara found all this alluring, sort of sexy and funny, but Sam didn't have a way to laugh about it yet. Barbara wanted to teach her. It needed to be laughed about, and plus Barbara had a little crush on Sam and wasn't ashamed of it. It was something she'd learned was normal, partly from reading Anne Frank's diary. It was something she was comfortable exploring. It maybe even felt a little mandatory. This was the reasonable thing to do at her age, Barbara knew that.

During cross-country practice Barbara would make Sam stretch her. Barbara was completely lean and at least five nine. She'd told Sam she'd done catalogue modeling in New York, and even though Sam was certain she was lying, they both thought she could have, if she tried.

"They like me to do underwear spreads because I have an ass for days," Barbara told her, turning around, showing her week-long ass, giving it a smack.

"That's great," Sam said.

Barbara would lie on her back and have Sam push her legs all the way forward until her ankles were by her ears and their noses were practically touching. Of course the eroticism wasn't wasted on Barbara, a child of academics. She knew everything there was to know well before she needed to. But Sam didn't know how to describe it, then, this impulse she had. Barbara would have to tell her later. At the time it just felt like eating, and it took all of Sam's will not to tear at Barbara's flesh with her teeth.

"This is how I do it when I do it," Barbara claimed, her ankles touching her earlobes.

Sam backed off a little. "You don't do it with anybody," she said, but Barbara insisted she had a boyfriend named Langston whom she'd met at summer camp. They supposedly had a lot of sex, but Sam was around so often she couldn't believe it was true, plus he never called. Really Barbara had thought him up to see if Sam would say something about Alfredo Brown, a boy whom Sam had supposedly been caught fucking in one of the project's communal basements. Sam was never home anymore, and Barbara should

have known it was a lie, but she couldn't let the story go. She wanted details. Did it hurt? How big was it? Was he good? Sam said nothing.

"My turn to stretch you," Barbara said.

"I don't want you to," Sam told her. "You're gonna hurt me."

"Come on." She lowered Sam down on the ground and grabbed her ankles. "Just imagine I'm Alfredo sticking his big black cock in you."

"You're disgusting," Sam said.

She pushed Sam's legs toward her head. Sam wasn't nearly as flexible as Barbara was, and it did hurt.

"My mom's making flank steak tonight," Barbara said. "You gonna pretend it's Alfredo's big black cock and eat the whole thing?"

"I'm not speaking to you for the rest of the day," Sam pouted.

"Oh come on, I'm just teasing." Barbara freed one of her hands from Sam's ankles and flicked Sam's crotch playfully. Sam kicked her away and told her she was nuts, but Barbara just cackled and began rolling around on the grass, flailing like a flipped turtle. Sam stood over her and shook her head. Sex hadn't crept into her consciousness yet, at least not deliberately. She was a late bloomer.

"You almost done there, asshole?" Sam asked. She extended a hand and helped Barbara to her feet.

After school Barbara's brother got them so high they couldn't move. Steven dealt pot and smoked blunts in his bedroom. He was the darker of the two kids, a distinction Steven and Barbara made and one Mr. and Mrs. Strauss diligently avoided. Steven was enthralled with his black heritage. He wore a big gold chain with an Africa-shaped pendant he'd found on eBay. He wrote rap songs about the Bronx, a mythological place he didn't remember. He played Buju Banton CDs and went to poetry slams in Central Square. Recently he'd decided he wanted to grow dreadlocks, and now the dome of his head looked like a neatly divided grid of Tootsie Roll tops. He sat on the floor in front of Sam and asked her to get the section of his head he couldn't reach. He gave her the aqua-colored goop he'd been twisting into his hair.

"This stuff smells really nice," Sam said.

"Yeah," Steven said, "It smells like how the ocean should smell, but doesn't."

Barbara watched Sam twist her brother's hair, watched her greasy fingers twirl and kink Steven's dense curls, and she thought she saw Sam smile a little: a sexy little smile, a flirty, dirty little smile, and she couldn't take it. Barbara grabbed Sam's hand and inhaled the green stuff flamboyantly. "This is *grrreat!*" she growled. "Just like the ocean, mmm!" She took Sam's hand and used it to smear the residue on her own head, a wave of processed, mother-bought ringlets. She pressed Sam's palm tight on her scalp and stared at her for a second too long, intently. It was the way Barbara always looked at Sam, not really accusation but interrogation; it was a look that was meant to get at the heart of the matter, the nitty-gritty, the truth, like she knew something that Sam didn't but needed Sam to know it soon.

"Langston thinks we spend too much time together," Barbara said. "He's getting suspicious."

"Of what?" Sam asked.

Steven and Barbara laughed to each other, laughed at Sam.

"I testify," Steven offered. "She sleeps in the Trombone Suite, undisturbed."

Sam was embarrassed. Her face began to feel hot and tight. She wanted to go home, but then she realized she didn't want to go home at all.

"I'm so high, you guys," she confided, and this only provoked Barbara. She stared, she sucked coyly on her index finger, she put Sam's hand on her thigh and then just went for it, right in front of her brother, just full-on went for it and grabbed the back of Sam's head and planted one on her, tongue and all, until Steven pushed her away.

Barbara laughed. "She's wicked high. She's gonna freak out, look at her."

"So stop already," Steven said.

Sam crossed her arms and nodded in agreement. She was an awful tease, Sam felt awfully teased, felt the rapid onslaught of some primal teasing something-or-other, some cataclysmic thingamajig the likes of which she'd never felt, didn't know about, didn't believe in, and she couldn't fucking wait. She'd kissed once before on a dare, and Steven had made her shotgun blunts before, suck the smoke straight from his lips just to get close, but Sam was clueless, just verging on a clue. Sex didn't happen in her home, not like in the Strauss House. Here it

happened so fast they could pretend it hadn't happened at all, and they'd already moved onto other topics. Still, Barbara was intent on needling her point into Sam.

"Did you know Sam and Alfredo Brown had sex in her basement?" Barbara told Steven.

"Fuck off," Sam said. Steven just laughed.

"What?" Barbara asked.

"That boy is gay," Steven said. "Queer as a three-dollar bill."

"I don't believe you," Barbara said.

"Well, he may not be gay now, but he will be." Steven said. "Trust me."

"Whatever," Barbara said. "It doesn't matter to me. But Sam's clearly got the fever."

"That's retarded," Sam said. "You're the one with the fever."

Steven started laughing again, said to Sam, "That's not how the fever works."

Sam tucked herself under her servant quilt that night and wondered if she'd made up the kiss. She closed her servant eyes and tried to fall asleep, but they fluttered, wouldn't stay shut. Her servant mind wouldn't succumb, wouldn't slow down.

Barbara wasn't having the same doubts. She'd been tirelessly building to this moment for weeks. It had been a minute-by-minute investment and she wasn't going to let her chance pass by. She was just waiting. Mr. Strauss liked to pace the house until two in the morning most nights, thinking in no clear line. Barbara almost fell asleep waiting for him to go to his room. She was half dreaming, the kind of dream that starts as fantasy: there was Sam and she was nude and her father was somehow going to make a move before she could, but Barbara caught herself, shook awake, and crept fearlessly to the servant's quarters, up the servant's stairs, to the servant's bed, right beside her precious little servant. At first they were all hands, but not for long.

It went on like that straight through the winter. Sam may have asked, *What are you doing?* or she may have just thought to ask, and the thought was so big it pounded in her ears, and then the question changed, and the pounding changed. *What am I doing?* Sam asked, and Barbara showed her.

*　*　*

It was indoor-track season and Sam was throwing the shot put for the varsity team. She was one of the few that scored points, but the event seemed vulgar and the other girls so masculine that she felt out of place, though she wasn't out of place at all. Barbara ran the one-mile faster than most of the boys on the team. Sam would watch her and cheer her on. Everything about Barbara was long: her toes were long, her shins were long, her neck, what a fucking neck!—and everything looked longer and leaner when she did the races. Her legs were flawless pistons. Eventually Sam noticed she wasn't the only one who noticed. Alfredo Brown was on the team. He did the long jump and the hurdles and, rumor was, he liked to compare sizes in the boys' locker room, but it seemed to her he spent most of his time bothering Barbara. *He's so gay*, Sam whispered to herself. Sam worried, Sam fumed, Sam flung her shot put twenty-five feet and the whole team cheered.

After practice they were sitting on the servant bed, servant-style, sharing orange sections and comparing physical imperfections. Sam had a large birthmark on her chest, almost like a wine stain. Barbara had bunions and wore a special foot brace at night that looked like a vice. Things were peaceful, ordinary. But quite suddenly the atmosphere in the room seemed to change. Their bodies felt heavier. Barbara's was especially affected. She sighed with boredom and turned to Sam deviously.

"I gave Alfredo Brown a blow job," Barbara claimed. "In the basement stairwell during free period."

"I don't believe you," Sam said.

"Well, I haven't done it yet, but I'm going to."

"Why?" Sam asked. "What's the point?"

"I don't know," Barbara said, "I just want to. Are you jealous? If you don't want me to, I won't."

"Fine then," Sam said. "I don't want you to."

"Why not?" Barbara said.

"Because I just don't," Sam said. "Because I love you and I just don't want you to."

Barbara wasn't prepared for this. They hadn't talked about love before, and though it made Barbara feel giddy

SKUPUJEMY SKÓRY ZWIERZĄT ŁOWNYCH

at first, the giddiness quickly turned to nausea. And then she couldn't help but feel a little angry with Sam for bringing it up.

"You can do it too, if you want," Barbara said. "We can do it together."

"That's disgusting," Sam said.

"I told him about us and he thinks it's hot," Barbara said. "He wants to come home with us after school sometime."

"You're an asshole," Sam said.

Barbara told her not to be so sensitive. Gave her a little kiss, a little tickle. And this was all it took. Barbara hadn't given Sam the tools of resistance. Sam couldn't say no to something she wanted.

They stayed in the servant's room and did their history homework. It always seemed to Sam that Barbara already knew all of it, as if her family had implanted all these facts in her brain during infancy. Sam knew nothing, and what she did know she didn't know that well, not like Barbara, who had living, working recall. Everything in her mind was useful, used for some ends. She could name all the popes in chronological order and list two facts each about their reigns and somehow explain how these distant events told us who we were today. Like Pope Leo, for instance: how he struck while the iron was hot, had his finger on the pulse, how he just took what he wanted; how he made the king kneel to him, and how the king conceded some powers in hopes of salvaging others; how they were two sides of the same coin. The only reason Sam could remember the date of the Magna Carta was because it was Barbara's birthday.

They were lucky they had history homework, because when Mrs. Strauss came home early, Steven got caught smoking. Normally they would have been in there with him. Mrs. Strauss had become paranoid about in-house illicit happenings. She was a mop-topped wrecking ball, perspiring and shrieking through the hallways, sprinting up the stairs.

"Who's smoking dope in my house!" she screamed, slamming doors. "So help me god, Steven, I will wring your neck!"

Barbara couldn't help but laugh at that one. *Why, I'll wring yer neck*, she mimicked. The two of them stayed shut in the servant's quarters, waited for the storm to pass.

Mrs. Strauss flung doors open and shrieked and shrilled, her face purple, her hairline mapped in beads of sweat. It was serious. She screamed his name.

Steven opened the door before she did. "What, Ma?" Steven said.

"Don't 'What Ma' me, Steven! You're smoking dope in my house and I'm not going to stand for it!"

"It's only pot, Ma. Can't a brother catch a break?" Steven said.

Mrs. Strauss gave Steven a smack upside the head, said, "Can't a motha get some peace?" and smacked him again. Steven was at least a foot taller than his mother, but he didn't feel that way. He felt tiny, miniature, microscopic in her presence.

"One more time! I catch you one more time and you're out of here!"

There was always the threat of being put out.

There's a joke they tell about Steven, Barbara told Sam. A family joke that he didn't like. The story goes he was three years old when they brought him home and he didn't want to be there. He ran to the squirrel room and hid and it's such a big house that nobody could find him for hours. When they did find him he was crying and shivering behind an antique sofa that had been reupholstered with porcupine quills. It was a dangerous sofa, and Steven had nicks all along his knees and forearms, defensive wounds. Because of this they likened him to a new car that turned out to be a lemon. Mr. Strauss would say, "We really should have purchased the warranty." That was the punch line. That joke always made Steven cringe. It made Barbara cringe. It gave Sam a nasty taste in her mouth. It was a bad joke.

By this time Barbara didn't bother sneaking anymore. She flagrantly, defiantly went to the servant's quarters, even on the nights when her father stood in the hallway keeping watch. Mr. and Mrs. Strauss were growing suspicious of their children's behavior, forever wafting air under their noses, searching for the faint odor of marijuana smoke. Mr. Strauss was by the attic staircase, crouching and sniffing, when Barbara approached.

"Go to bed, Dad," Barbara said.

Mr. Strauss bowed his head, said "Yessum," like he imagined Aunt Jemima would.

Barbara tiptoed up the stairs. The lights were on. Sam was servant-flossing in bed, and servant-moisturizing her skin because Barbara had told her she was getting ashy. It was a dry winter. It was a dry bed. It was a dry dinner of matzo and pickled beets and dry, stringy pulled pork. Something was off-kilter. Sam was hot to the touch, confused, and Barbara wasn't giving any direction. Sam toed Barbara's braced foot, played footsie, tried to take charge, but Barbara backed away, edged to her side of the bed and stared at the ceiling fan, stared at the blades slicing the ham bone of the servant's quarters' servant air. It was time to face some facts, Barbara told Sam.

"What do you mean, we need to face some facts?" Sam asked.

Barbara tilted her head and took a long, thoughtful breath. She looked to Sam like she was putting on airs, performing.

"Do you really think you love me?" Barbara asked.

"Sure, why not?" Sam pulled at her hair nervously. "What's the problem?"

"I'm not sure," Barbara said. "I just think we might have outgrown each other."

Sam was unprepared for this. She felt the very opposite of what Barbara described. In fact, she'd almost come to imagine the two of them as a single entity, growing together, not outgrowing each other. They were a *thing*, a solid, organic *thing*, like a tree or a plant, and Sam hadn't come to question its half-life. She put her hand along Barbara's panty line, tried to get her going, but Barbara shoved Sam's hand away.

"Not even a little?" Sam asked.

"No," Barbara said. "But we can spend tonight together."

Barbara didn't clarify, and Sam wasn't sure, but it sounded to Sam like she was being put out, which meant she'd have to go home, which really was a place Sam had given up, outgrown.

"I'm probably going to give Alfredo Brown a blow job tomorrow, and then I'm probably going to make him my boyfriend," Barbara said.

"Oh," Sam said. "No, but—I said I didn't want you to."

"It's really not up to you," Barbara said, coolly, cruelly.

"But what about this? What about what we do?"

"Well," Barbara said, "it'll probably be hard at first, but we'll get over it. I'm sorry. It's just the way it has to be."

Sam began to twitch. She ticked. "But this seems like a choice," she said.

"It's not one I'm making lightly. I've been deliberating for days now," Barbara said.

"You could have told me," Sam said. "We could have deliberated about it together."

"Oh dear," Barbara said. "I forget sometimes how much you like me." She put her arms around Sam and held her like a puppy.

Sam started crying. She called Barbara an asshole and turned away, but she couldn't keep from letting Barbara hold her from behind.

"I'm not proud of it," Barbara said. And that was true. She was just trying not to go crazy. She knew her life only allowed for so much deviance. "It's like when I was a little kid. I feel like one half of me hates the other."

Sam seethed. She couldn't quite grasp the situation. Her throat felt filled with salt. "Well," she said, "maybe that half has a good reason."

"I'm trying to tell you something," Barbara started, but caught herself. "But maybe you're too stupid to get it."

"Probably am," Sam said. "Now why don't you go fuck yourself."

Barbara spooned up behind her and slept. And wept. And Sam cried too, held Barbara's fingers tight against her chest and cursed her. Barbara was thinking about her family. This was the reasonable thing, she told herself. It was better for all of them if she just let Sam go.

There was still the matter of Alfredo's big black cock. And this is what Sam couldn't stop thinking about. That treacherous instrument, it swirled and stretched and hissed, and in her nightmare-fantasies it strangled her. She'd been had, duped, and now she was out of the loop. Barbara was keeping something from her, a secret, a big secret, and it was meant solely for her and Alfredo, and Sam felt dead, but not dead: she felt like she'd been murdered, but she wasn't dead, she was still too present. Sam felt a ghostly mania from

within, and this must have been it, that moment when she would go crazy, but she wasn't sure and that was the scary part. She felt a torrent, a tempest, a torrential downpour of globular phantom eggs, little spheres of condensed aloneness, bits of her mother and father pelting her in the face. It was a horrible secret, the one Barbara had shown her, the one about being alone and not knowing it, then being-with and loving it, then being-with but feeling alone and wanting to crawl out of her skin. Then being just alone. It was a horrible betrayal, and it wasn't something Sam could see herself laughing about someday. The Strauss House jokes were never very funny.

There was no sleeping for Sam; maybe there would never be any sleep again, like for her father, or maybe there'd be sleep all the time, like for her mother. She hadn't seen them since the fall, since she'd moved into the servant's quarters and become a prospective punch line, one Mr. and Mrs. Strauss would tell to new guests at the dinner table once Sam wasn't there to hear it and hate it. Sam nudged Barbara, but she was out cold. Little flakes of salt crusted down her tear line, and Sam licked these flakes, tasted the salt, and Barbara snarled a little but still didn't wake. "I hate you," Sam whispered. "I want to kill you." Sam stood over Barbara and waited for something to happen, but nothing did. The world felt utterly static. The only things in motion were Sam's own thoughts. She imagined herself shrunken to the size of a fist, small enough to fit inside Barbara's mouth. Sam thought it would be nice if she could crawl inside there and live quietly until she died. She ruminated on this image until it made her nauseous and the sight of Barbara's mouth suddenly enraged her. Sam knew it was time to leave. She fled from her servant's bed, tramped across the servant's rugs, trotted down the servant's stairs, and set out for her house. Mr. Strauss was in the pantry without any pants, working on his dissertation, staring at a slide of a seven-foot-tall statue of Min, the Egyptian penis god.

Mr. Strauss spotted her, said, "Oh, Samuel, have I told you about the penis god?"

Sam said, "You and your penis god can go fuck in hell."

"Right-ee-o," Mr. Strauss said. He thought it might be an interesting thesis.

It was a long walk home. It was a very long walk home.

The Land of Our Enemies

NATHANIEL MINTON

I

Peterson did everything by the book. For instance, he did not, like the man Freyman, strap on a parachute and jump from the plane when the left engine caught fire. No, Peterson took the throttle and yoke and attended to the serious business of a crash landing. The plane was, after all, filled with valuable cargo—guns and gold and Bibles—and Peterson was not a man to let the tools of civilization die without a fight.

A plane like a Beech Twin has two engines for a reason, and Peterson knew how to fly with one. But the plane wouldn't stay up without fuel, and the left-engine fire was burning through his supply. There was a thin layer of sweat on his palms; he wiped it off and brought the plane close enough to the jungle canopy for the right propeller to mince leaves and branches into a pulp that stuck to the cockpit windows.

Freyman was the pilot. Freyman was also a ruffian, a cad, and a ne'er-do-well, so remembering him as the pilot was a certain kindness on the part of Peterson. Freyman, if still on board, would have jettisoned the concrete and steel that nearly filled the hold, but Peterson had other plans for his resources. If he had been gifted with foresight he would have built a runway in the rainforest, but it was night and there were no clearings and when the right wing caught on the vegetation the aircraft wrestled itself from Peterson's hands and he woke up with two broken ribs.

II

Freyman survived his jump in true RAF form. On that first night he strangled an anteater to death with one hand while lighting a fire with the other. He used a knife to cut out its genitals, removed the musk glands to avoid tainting the flesh, then sliced the hide from neck to tail and peeled it back to keep the hair from the meat. He split the sternum and, cutting the gullet and windpipe, removed the intestines, stomach, and internal organs. He cut a circle around the anus and pulled it through the body cavity. He cooked and ate the meat. He drained the blood and drank it. He burned the entrails.

He used his knife to chisel through several small trees and vines by resting the blade horizontally on the trunk and hammering the dull edge with a rock. He built a platform in the low crook of a dying tree and sheltered it with a cut section of the parachute. He thought little of the future. He acted with little reason because a man needs little reason to survive. A man needs a knife and a source of clean water and freedom from pain, and when those comforts are secure he can perhaps reflect for a moment on his circumstances, on the vagaries of rescue, on the necessity of civilization, and, if he is lucky, upon the kinds of love a family feels for a hobo son, or the satisfying human rituals of movement and settlement.

A plane is not a ship and the captain doesn't go down with it. Maybe Peterson had more resources at his disposal, but were those resources really necessary? Was a man really dependent on books and bullets? Freyman didn't think so. He told himself, "A man doesn't need a city like a city needs a man," and he dried the anteater ribs, carved holes in a length of solid rainforest hardwood, lined the ribs up in the holes, and played them like a xylophone until he had composed a sonata in F minor.

Later he left his platform and climbed the tallest tree he could find. He brought the parachute with him and strung a hammock out of it. He caught birds with his bare hands and stole fruit from monkeys and when he slept, he slept like a man who had never known quiet, and had never experienced peace, but had not forgotten how to dream, because he was two hundred and nine feet tall with legs of telmocite, veins of diamond tributary, and hands forged from the solid iron core of firmament. He felt strong, healthy, calm. He wasn't lonely.

When the natives found him and surrounded his tree, Freyman did not climb down. He didn't want any trouble, and he tried to make that clear by not exposing his teeth and by slumping his shoulders as if he were weeping. He tried speaking to them, but their primitive minds couldn't comprehend the intricacies of language. Freyman supposed they had some rudimentary form of communication, but he knew it would make little difference. To them he was simply something foreign, and foreign objects need to be

rejected in much the same way his mother's new kidney had been. Before long they shot arrows at him.

But Freyman was not a parasite, was not symbiotic, was not a colonial power; he was nothing, not a disturbance, not an irritant, not a malignant cell trying to convert others to his corrupted genetic code. That was Peterson's job. That was why he had paid Freyman to bring him to this dissolute and fecund patch of untouched culture in the first place. That was why Peterson went down with the plane and Freyman didn't.

If only they had understood all this, he could have lived up there for years, collecting rain in monkey skulls and ruminating on the nature of man, instead of grimly pissing on the fire they lit at the base of his tree. They were not trying to smoke him out—the tree was green and wet and would not burn. The savages were smart. Smart enough not to climb up there after him, smart enough not to waste more arrows, smart enough to weaken the wood until they could fell the tree instead. There were many of them and they had an immeasurable length of time to accomplish their task and they would succeed.

They only needed eight days. They burned the base, scraped away the charcoal with sharpened stones, and set their flames to the underlying flesh. They did this twice a day and it undermined the structure of the tree enough that Freyman, with the use of vines, was forced to create supports for the trunk, triangulating it between its three nearest neighbors. He had the idea that when the savages finally broke through, the trunk would stutter and shift from the stump and perhaps sink several feet, but it would not fall. That way they would have to start burning one of the support trees, and that process would give him time. He only wanted to maintain his platform.

Freyman turned out to be, by his own calculations, only about two-thirds right. He had perhaps failed to realize that, without roots, and subject to the length and leverage of a two-hundred-foot column of wet wood capped by a bundle of branches, trees are top-heavy. He had perhaps not tightened the support lines sufficiently, or had not accounted for the pushing of twenty-five savages who cheered and screamed when the first vine broke.

III

Peterson, because he had a considerable supply of morphine, was able to ignore the pain in his broken ribs. With the building materials he salvaged from the Beech Twin he built himself an enduring structure with three rooms and constructed a wall around it. He reinforced the wall with carbonized bamboo, fortified it with sharpened stakes, and read the Book out loud. With the initial encystment complete, he began work on a second structure, a post-and-lintel lavatory with walls of stretched hide, and so it was that he plowed the earth with his hands and cut his last potato and buried each eye in the dark soil beside the mangled plane, and the earth was blessed with the sacrament of his seed, and the fruit of the earth was blessed, and blessed was Peterson in his field, for he kept his covenant, realized the inevitability of intervention, and dug a two-foot hole in the dirt. He took a length of pipe from the left engine and inserted it into the earth at an angle to the hole. Once he cleared the soil from the pipe it provided excellent ventilation for the fire. He kept embers burning in the hole as he slept, the green wood smoldering through the darkness to be stoked in the gray dawn, stoked into ascendant flames that caressed and sterilized a half-empty can of Vienna sausages.

Over time he burned a hundred acres around the camp and churned the ash into the soil with the circular power of the right engine attached to wheels and geared down to earth-tilling speed. He planted corn and wheat and eggplant and carved his own likeness on the side of nine trees encircling his civilization. At night he closed the bamboo gates, shut himself in his concrete home, and shivered himself to frightful sleep because he was a coward.

IV

The convicts came from the ocean. They were orphaned when their ship, the *Amaziah*, broke apart on the rocky Western Cliffs. It took them forty days to reach Peterson. They stood outside the city walls as Peterson looked down on them from the parapets. Sunburned and battered, in threadbare jumpsuits, they pleaded

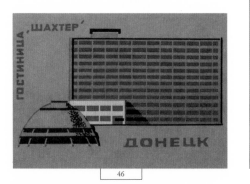

from the gates. "We're hungry," they called. "Look at us. Look at us! We have eaten our stores and our dead. We don't know how to survive out here. We need food."

"Who speaks for you?" Peterson said. "Which one of you leads the others?"

They shuffled their bare feet and shot glances around the group. Some of them mumbled a name or two but not one man spoke up or stepped forward.

"Who among you can use a hammer and saw?"

One man stepped forward. "I can, sir."

Peterson opened the gate and let the man in. His name was Minsky, and his head was bald and he had a friendly grin and hands the size of his face. Peterson shut the gate behind him, shook the man's hand, led him to the commissary, and provided a meal of stale cornbread and protein-rich maggots pulled from the gangrenous leg of a capybara and sautéed with garlic and monkey butter. Minsky thought about each bite. He ate slow. When he was finished, he pushed his bowl to the side and looked at Peterson.

"I am grateful to you, sir," he said. "There are people in this world without a drop of genuine charity in their souls. I'm from California," he winked, "so I know what I'm talking about. I used to be one of them, in fact. I killed my whole family with a golf club and did other things too but here we are in the middle of hell and you just fed me the best meal I've had in months so the way I see things I owe you."

"This is a kindness," Peterson said. "You owe me nothing."

"That's where you're dead wrong according to me, Minsky, because I owe you one meal's worth of carpentry. What do you need built?"

"I need a keep."

"What's a keep?"

"The final refuge of civilization."

"So you're one of those who believe in Jesus?" Minsky asked.

"I am."

"Yeah," Minsky said. "Me too. That's good. So you'll keep feeding me?"

"I will."

"Quid pro quo?"

"Just kindness," Peterson told him, and he rendered chunks of animal fat over a small fire, mixed in the watery ash he had strained

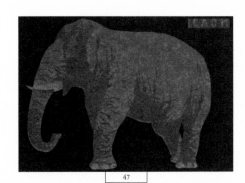

through a bandanna in a one-to-two ratio, and set the container aside to cool. He boiled pots of water and added them to the rainwater in the concave basin of a bisected fuel tank. He set a simple shirt and woolen pants by the tub, carved soap from the bucket, handed Minsky a towel, and turned his back while the man bathed.

Minsky looked around at Peterson's muddy camp, the rusting plane, the outhouse, the creaking table, the walls he'd built, and he said, "It's good here, isn't it?"

"I'm just getting started," Peterson said. "I'm going to build a real church."

The convicts sang in the evenings because God is a mighty fortress amid the flood of mortal ills. Peterson brought them Bibles and in the days that followed they cheered every inch that Minsky's keep emerged above the walls, believing that their songs were somehow sinking into the earth and rising up within the city as a tower of devotion.

Among them Peterson found a thieving blacksmith who had branded himself for his own sins, and he brought him through the gates. The man built a forge and hammered out strong iron bars to reinforce the new walls intended to encircle the residential area of the city. A tax-evading mason trained three men to press and dry the river clay and when they brought a hundred thousand bricks to him Peterson let them in and they laid firm road between the buildings. In the evening they built houses to the sounds of old-time religion swaying through the trees.

The conical nose of the plane was hung in the hinge of a lewis, with a carved anteater skull for a clapper, and Peterson rang that bell as the last convict crossed the city threshold to witness the final nail driven into The Keep and Minsky's smiling mug as he descended by block and tackle to the city streets. The last convict lit the streetlights and Peterson declared it a holiday and the vintners brought flagons of wine and the bakers brought cakes of raisins and there was much jubilation for each and all from the lonely counterfeiter to the disgruntled clerk.

Such great strides they had made in so short a time! How eloquently they had prevailed upon nature! How safe they felt inside their shuttered walls and battened minds!

V

Freyman was a beneficiary of the kind of providence that presents itself through certain topographical and geological formations, in this case by way of the small hollow time had carved below him with erosion and deposition, and into which his body fell, unmangled, uncrushed, and unconscious.

The natives cut through his parachute cord with sharpened rocks and carried him back to their village, where they laid him in a pit of excrement. In the morning the men took turns beating him with bamboo canes and by afternoon the excrement had infected the bleeding welts of those lashings and Freyman found himself in a feverish state. The heat of his body boiled his own fluids and also the puddle of vile liquid in which his crumbled body burned. The fluids turned to vapor and rose above the pit to meet the dew point of cooler air and condense into a stinking cloud that swept on gentle breezes through the jungle and rained down Freyman's tears upon the earth.

They left his quivering heap to die in the pit. Their actions were dictated not by careful thought or reasoned planning but by superstitious caution and base instinct. But he sweated the fever out and it made him stronger; it hardened him. He climbed from the pit and walked naked through the jungle. Wet leaves bathed his skin and healed his wounds and left him with a lustrous glow that emerged from within his flesh. He was good, and he was clean, and he had lost his capacity for anger, feeling, thought.

He went back into the natives' village and drank their water and ate their food, and when they returned they surrounded him with spears and chanted savage songs of fear and hate. But their weapons produced no blood from his flesh, and they believed that a man who does not bleed is perhaps not a man at all but something else. Much yelling and discussion followed, and more prodding and attempts to cut him, but he could not be cut. Eventually they called for the Chief, a man with seven generations of grandchildren, who had guided the village through hopes and woes with a steady hand and faith in tradition, which told him that life was both sacred and expendable. He could look so deep into another man's eyes that he saw all that man's past lives stacked like

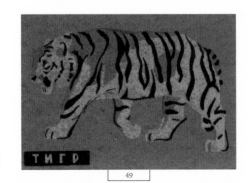

ТИГР

helical vertebrae in a descending line to the great ancestral creation day, but his belly was round and stuck out beneath his ribs and his teeth were rotten and he was a mean little troll. He poked Freyman with his befouled finger, and he pulled his ears, and he put his hand in Freyman's mouth. He pulled at Freyman's penis and smelled him all over. In Freyman's eyes he saw the certainty of mourning and he shouted to his tribesmen and they scurried off like ants about their village. They hastened back with wood and fire, and they set about erecting a stake for the burning of Freyman.

It is difficult to blame Freyman for what happened next.

VI

Freyman stuck his bare arm down the Chief's throat, tearing through the esophageal tissue and releasing a torrent of blood skyward. He wrapped his formidable mitt around the man's heart, which he squeezed until it stopped beating and the Chief fell to the ground, shed from Freyman's bloody arm like the desiccated skin of a snake.

The savages were astonished.

Freyman dispatched the next man who approached with a swift punch to the throat, crushing his windpipe and rendering him useless to the living for any purpose beyond ceremony. The third man he tore limb from limb. The fourth he skinned alive and took his hide to wear as an overcoat. Freyman did all this because he had the ability to do so, and because his time with the villagers had awakened in him a desire to exploit his initiative. The fifth man begged for mercy and threw himself to the ground, in awe that Freyman had risen before them, a vicious and victorious man whose anger would transform their wills, strengthen their families, and return them home.

The others ran for their lives. He chased them in his bloody clothing through the vine and scrabble of their old world. He tracked them to their hiding places and he did to them as he found occasion, and those who acquiesced at the sight of him found some mercy at his hands and joined the first beggar in the village center, where the afternoon light came upon them in scattered orange shafts cut from the smoke of cooking fires. Freyman sat

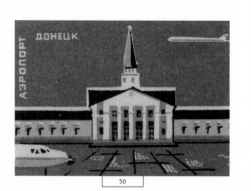

down in front of the beggar and spoke to him. He named the man Judgment Day and the jungle was silent.

When Freyman rose, Judgment Day rose with him, and when Freyman walked, Judgment Day walked beside him. In the evening they dined on the flesh of the fallen and honored them in the traditional manner, and when they had their fill the beggars performed for Freyman a dance in which animals fought one another and died to be eaten by man. Freyman considered the imperatives that drove him now and knew that some among their number would be sacrificed. He knew his heart was strong and hungry. When Freyman slept, Judgment Day slept with him.

In the morning Freyman laid a rock, a spear, and a bow before them. He sat with Judgment Day and examined the three objects. He reached first for the bow and Judgment Day beat him to it, grasping the weapon in his own hand. Freyman withdrew his hand and the man released the bow. He repeated the process with the spear but did not so much reach as indicate with his hand the direction of the spear and once again the man snatched it up.

By the afternoon, Freyman could think of the rock but move for the spear and Judgment Day would pick up the rock. They had reached a level of nonverbal communication whereby the unconscious tensing of certain muscles indicated desire more than a command ever could. Judgment Day smiled, and when Freyman embraced him he embraced Freyman, and when Freyman cut himself and showed Judgment Day the true nature of his mortal blood the man was grateful and understood the passion of their duality was rooted in knowing that tides have no motive beyond gravity.

In the following days three more beggars took positions on Freyman's compass. Judgment Day trained them and when they were ready Freyman gave them names. In front was Melas and behind was Leukos and at his left was Thanatos and when Freyman turned they all turned with him.

They came upon the neighboring village at dawn. They came thundering as one, Judgment Day on the right with five men to follow his actions and Thanatos on the left with another five. Melos had six in front, two lookouts,

a tracker, a man who called out battle cries that split the hearts of their enemies, and two blind men with ears so acute they could hear a tree falling in the woods two days before it happened. Leukos took up the rear with another ten men in two groups of five, one for each of Freyman's toes.

They came upon the village with a precision and a might usually reserved for higher predators. They came with singular intent, and they took their spoils to feed their women and children, and Freyman ate twenty-nine tapirs and the lean nutrition of his meal fed every man in every branch and limb. They grew stronger and took seven more villages in as many weeks. Of those opponents who survived, the strong were absorbed into the body politic of the Freymen, and the weak were left to wander the jungle in search of shoots and insects, and the weakest of those, in desperation, answered the ring of a distant bell and found themselves one pleasant afternoon begging for scraps outside the walls of a small city and taken in as refugees. In the evening they told their tragic stories and cried as the convicts looked on, waiting hungrily for this spectacular opportunity to manifest itself in a new labor class that would take their place at unskilled tasks and elevate the convicts to the rank of soldiers and priests and doctors and scholars.

Peterson watched as the cooking fires of his society rested in embers for the night. He prayed the fortifications could withstand their dread. He kissed the ground of his concrete bunker and prayed for the refugees and their children, for the second-story men, and for those who never came to the Kingdom of God. Then he waited.

VII

When they saw the towering visage of Peterson carved deep into a hundred trees the Freymen recognized him before Freyman did, but the message traveled quickly. When it reached him Freyman took swift and deliberate action, directing his arms to sink into the earth and begin digging toward the city. He had two hundred and six men in his skeletal system alone, twenty-seven bones in each hand, and each reported along a chain of command that ran right up to Thanatos and Judgment Day, who took

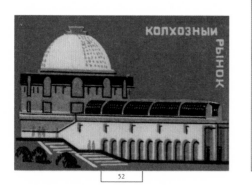

their cues from Freyman and scurried their men into the ground like tunneling rodents. Freyman breathed deep and pressed through rock and clay and if his hands bled he bled with them.

Thanatos got his hand through first. He found a refugee sleeping in the city square and popped his head off with a flick of his thumb. He flattened a barking dog with a decisive swat. The noise woke the convicts and they in turn woke Peterson, who unlocked the doors of the armory and passed out rifles in the orderly fashion of a civilized man, two men to each gun so if one was killed the other could pick up the weapon and keep fighting. They aimed first at the screaming natives who invaded from the Western Wall, firing mercilessly with grins as wide as their murderous nature. They saw no hand but a teeming mass of thirty or forty men who fought in a manner that both confused and frightened them. They had heard of these men from the refugees, and now they put their bullets to work.

Their shots stung Freyman like the malicious needles of a band of tropical medicos. Freyman lost the first joint of his left thumb and index finger and began to bleed badly. He grabbed at a small group of convicts and fought through the pain that surged up when he closed his fist around them, then shook their pulped flesh from his hand and withdrew it past the wall to heal. He left the dying men of his fingertips behind, replacing them with a clump of hair instantly retrained. And the pain melted away, and by and by he felt whole once again, and Judgment Day smashed through the East Wall and shot toward the backs of another group of city men, who were still staring at the bloody tear to the west with a sense of minor victory that lasted precisely as long as their lives.

Peterson was bunkered in a steel and concrete basement; eye slats at ground level allowed him to see most of the city. As the fighting went on he unrolled a map of their defenses on a plank table and, using all the knowledge he had gained from following a book, devised a counterattack. He knew the walls were too bootless to protect them; thus salvation lay in war. He armed Minsky and six pedophiles with Gatling guns and machetes and sent them to the battle.

Judgment Day was in up to the elbow when a thousand burning bullets shattered through Freyman's upper radius and ulna,

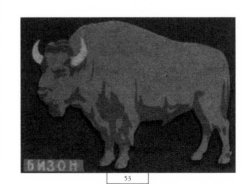

БИЗОН

amputating his right hand and forearm in one quick cut. All thirty-two of Freyman's teeth clenched against one another as Judgment Day withdrew the bloody stump. It would not heal so easily as a few flesh wounds and finger joints. While what remained of his arm was hacked apart by convict blades, Freyman raised himself on the backs of a thousand men. Standing, he looked down upon the city.

VIII

The muscle that circulated blood and oxygen and life through the Freymen's body was not built from the flesh of men but from the xylophonic bones of an anteater. It was the fine notes and rhythms of that instrument that drove his passion and his humors, and it was the exquisite intuition of its melodies that fueled the engine of his will. When he stood, his heartbeat rang through the town with a vital clarity that silenced every screeching and stirring creature in earshot. It was his heart, his monstrous heart that struck fear in their ditheistic souls.

So Peterson raised an arrow at Freyman's heart, a burning canister of trinitro-toluene attached to the shaft, and loosed the explosive might of chemistry upon the pericardium of men who guarded that pure music. The precision ordnance of Peterson's searing civilization eroded the men with grotesque efficiency. It was the second arrow that muffled the beat and brought Freyman to his knees. The third shattered every rib.

In the moments before his heart stopped beating, Freyman, in an act both just and desperate, ripped the remains of his right arm from the socket and flung it at Peterson. It was in this way that Judgment Day visited the civilized man and eviscerated his skull with a single glance from his terrible swift sword.

The remaining convicts fled and the refugees fled and the Freymen fled and they took their dead and dying with them. Judgment Day ran alone into the darkening jungle to lie in wait for a thousand years. Two bodies and a burning city remained. Two bodies slumped on concrete and brick. And the fire reached Freyman and lifted his body unto the sky as

ZTÁLINVÁROS 1950 VI.- 1960 VI

smoke, and a lonely anteater wandered through the city, stopping only to relieve itself on the bloody corpse of Peterson before foraging off into the night.

IX

And the windows of heaven were opened and the first drops of rain washed away the urine and the blood and the bile. And the waters were a cleansing tonic that assuaged all fear and famine in the hearts of men. And the waters abated the anger and avarice of their minds. And the waters brought worms up from the soil to squiggle and squirm in the moistening air, and brought life to the plants that dismantled concrete and overspread the land with crawling limbs and leaf. And a twig was plucked from a branch by the beak of a dove and gave proof of the grace of the earth and of the oceans and of the skies above.

Augury

J. ERIN SWEENEY

When I was young and traveled a great deal, I once passed through a foreign land with a lovely local custom. I was staying in a small city perched on the edge of the Malay Peninsula, a place where large white peacocks roamed the public parks. The peacocks fascinated foreigners and travelers like myself, who sat on scrolled iron benches to feed them seeds and murmured with awe when they fanned their tails out wide. But in addition to the peacocks, the park also sustained and encouraged a semiferal population of lesser red-eared lorises.

The lorises were tree dwelling. Because of this, they were difficult to see in their entirety, but now and then they came down to gambol over the grass, from one patch of shade to another, before hoisting themselves back up into the branches and disappearing again. They were about the size of cats, with thick blue-gray fur spread out from a white corona around eyes set nerdishly close together, and when on the ground they had a rolling, bearlike gait that transferred the weight of their soft bodies from forelegs to hind and back. With clever fingers, they grasped the bits of bean bun and tiny fried sugarfish that were extended in a cupped hand or spilled on the ground in front of them. Back at home in Pennsylvania lorises were a rarity even in zoos, but here they were quite commonplace.

Even more unusual—to the delight of locals and visitors alike—the lorises had a tendency to offer unsolicited advice. Skeptics liked to say that their aphorisms were too cryptic and abstract to have any meaning at all, and some added that though the messages sounded personal, they could apply equally well to any audience. But this never deterred young couples from listening closely to the lorises, as they strolled the tree-lined paths hand in hand, and it lent a certain delightful augury to business transactions conducted in the open air.

I was first advised by a loris as I sat on a bench removing the paper wrapping from a bean bun I had purchased at a vendor's cart. I was told that excessive possessions weary the soul and that generosity is the way of the wise.

I looked up into the branches above me, from whence this advice had come. Two white-rimmed black eyes blinked down from the leaves. I tore a piece from my bun and held it up, hoping to lure my counselor into the open, where I could have a better look at him or her. But the motion of my arm was too sudden. The gap in the branches swung closed with a rattle of fan-shaped leaves. This loris, young and easily startled, had retreated to higher ground.

Amazed, I looked around to see who else had witnessed this. Only the bean-bun vendor who stood at his cart, watching me.

I hailed him in English.

How do I call them back? I asked.

The vendor's smile was broad and toothless.

Loris! he said. He pointed at the tree.

I know! I said.

A wildflower sky arched above us, eternal and cloud free.

Is loris!

He laughed.

And so did I, because this had never happened to me before and so I could not believe it and that is the way I react to things that I cannot believe.

I did not see that particular loris again. But I saw many more in the days that followed, because the loris is a thing of wonder and in this world, wonders abound. I stayed in the city for five days. By that time I had visited most of the local art galleries and white stone shrines I could find in my guidebook, and I was ready to move on. But when I boarded a bus bound for the coast, I had the first of a series of daydreams that I would nurture for the next three years—daydreams of bringing a few lorises home to Pennsylvania and letting them roam free in Rockville's central park. The climate might not suit them, but shelters could be built to ease the shock of winter. Food could be arranged. And Rockvillians would take their advice wisely, I thought. The people of my town would listen with open minds, a dash of restraint, and a healthy degree of good sense. We were, after all, decent humble people with simple expectations. And that was our way.

I am having trouble writing this, I'll be honest. My problem is that I'm newly in love, and thus my attention is divided between this fact and the requirements of my story. I am wondering what will become of me, and I'm living a life that nobody will ever examine or try to make sense of, whether I am here to explain myself or not. Three years after I returned from my travelings, and largely as a result of my own foray into civic activism, a few breeding pairs of lorises were imported and released into the park on the spear point of petitions, public interest, and easily raised funds. Nothing is perfect in Rockville, of course; the schools are rife with inadequate teaching and everywhere things are not getting done that perhaps should be getting done, butter spread thin on bread and money going where money ought not to go, etc. Things are not perfect in any town; I think we can agree on this. But once the idea had been put before them, the citizens of Rockville did not rest until the project had been seen through. These people—what can I say about them? They want what they want.

The lorises dispersed happily into the park. They took to the Rockville climate better than I imagined they would. Soon they were breeding and romping and frolicking all over the place. They thrived, living on the generosity of the land and protected through the winter by their thick roan pelts and accumulating blubber. They did well, and then too well. In time they were rustling within the trees like furry blue tumors, displacing native attitudes, spreading strange hope, strange stirrings. The way they decorated the skyline reminded me of gypsy moth caterpillars, the kind that devastate whole forests by building tents in the trees each spring and eating the branches bare by summer. Only they were worse in some ways because they offered people the possibility of something else outside of all this, something different, and they gave such thoughtful advice. That was the lure of what they said—it always came after careful reflection. They also enjoyed treats, like buttermilk biscuits from KFC, and people soon found that the warmer and more plentiful the biscuits, the longer the reflection would extend.

As they grew fatter, they became a bit oilier, and also clumsier—they fell out of the trees sometimes, which could be startling. But they were so happy! And they made us happy too. They told us to correct our ways. We had to try harder, we had to enjoy ourselves, we had to chill the fuck out. It twisted us around, this pleasure.

The pleasure of being told this. It was as satisfying as love, and as perverse. I should know, since as of lately I've experienced both.

Soon some of us began to suspect that things had gone too far. Groups of lorises had taken to gathering on the lawn of the capitol building, and the city had to employ specially trained border collies to round them up and chase them away. Taxes had to be raised to pay for the fleet of city workers hired to clean up the residue they left on golf courses, which we did not like to discuss. They raided garbage cans and tore up vegetable gardens. They made powerful friends. Meanwhile they ate. They bickered. They made up. They bred.

The zebra mussel creates trouble by clogging northeastern pipes and waterways. The kudzu grows a foot per day, isn't that right? And the snakehead fish just eats every living thing in its path and that is of course no good. The mitten crab simply doesn't belong here, and there's a jellyfish in New Jersey that is washing up on shores by the zillions. We do not want a zillion of anything, anywhere, and certainly not zillions of drifting clumps and clusters of stinging nonnative jellyfish. There are three unpleasant things, three things most discomforting to think about: the unusual, the insatiable, and the many. We can ask how they got here, and we can ask where they came from, but these are our questions, not theirs. I think it's safe to say that if they have a question at all, it's about what comes next.

That last one there—the New Jersey jellyfish situation—gave me an idea. Perhaps, in light of the events I had already set in motion, I should have paused before recklessly pursuing more ideas of this kind. But I didn't. Am I alone in preferring the feeling of clean hands to hands that are less than clean? Don't answer—I know that I'm not.

I had heard of a chef in Delaware who had been gathering up the jellyfish and exploring various means of cooking them—she had tried broiling, boiling, drying, curing, and deep-fat frying them in a range of curious and promising seasonings, with varying degrees of success. Her restaurant was locally famous, and thus her jellyfish experiments were much discussed, and that was

how I found her. We became friends after a fashion, two people bound by what they have done, or what they might do for the world in which they have found themselves, this world in which wonders abound. I had mistakes to set right, and she had a population to feed with elegance in exchange for money.

I drove out to see her on a snowy Wednesday in February. I miss the Malay Peninsula acutely in weather like this. The windshield wipers were beating away the flurries and slush rose in gray spatters from the wheels of the truck in front of me. I am going to tell you something rather hard to take now, but you must bear with me. This is what happened. I'm in love and it's after ten o'clock and at this hour I have no tolerance for dissembling. Something beside the road caught my attention.

I stopped the car and stepped out into a bleak wet landscape, a frozen gray place where it is not good to be alone or to die. In any other town, the furry heap half covered in driven snow might have been a cat or a raccoon, but that was less likely here. I poked the dead loris with my foot and found it intact. A better word would be fresh, probably, but that word did not suit my circumstances. I was wearing a fisherman's sweater and a wool coat, standing under a blank white sky heavy with its own kind of portent. I worked for a medical publishing company. I had two nephews and I played the violin. I pried the loris free from the frozen ground and wrapped it in an old blanket, which I carried to the car in my arms and placed in the trunk. When I arrived at Chez Maria's it had almost thawed.

She welcomed me inside. Over tea, she explained that since the last time we had talked she had procured samples of zebra mussels, some species of bees, invasive weeds of all kinds, the eggs of birds we know too well, and a dozen other lifeless creatures who never belonged here and who chose their fate and circumstances the same way we all do, which is to say not at all. They were in her walk-in freezer. But to date, nothing had arisen from any of her culinary experiments that had approached the delicious, or even the edible. What does a quail have that a plump starling doesn't? She couldn't say, but it was something.

On a stainless-steel table in her prep room, we examined the loris, which she had deftly washed and skinned. It lay in reddish repose, humiliated and dismembered, shining and wet.

A good chef occupies a world in which rightness hangs like a ham between the brutish and the honest. There is thought and there is food, and what the two have in common with each other is what the chef shares with people like you and me. Everything necessary occupies a tremorous, fragile space between everything else; if I enjoy the food in front of me without regard for its origins, if I believe I have friends, if I find myself in love, it is largely because of what I don't know, and I have to accept this. There is nothing grotesque or peaceful in the world except that which is both. A loris told me this. Anyway. My friend lifted a hind leg and thrust her knife in, which took some effort. Then she slid the blade down along the… well, she did her work, as a chef will do. She studied at the French schools. We dropped small pieces of the loris into hot oil and tried them with seven different sauces lined up in little white bowls.

I was not too put off by the fourth one, which tasted like peanuts. But in her assessment, they were all terrible. Not without promise, maybe. But she would need to fuss with this. She would need to think it over. I was more than happy to let her keep the carcass. I joked that it was a gift. In the spirit of the gift I had given the town of Rockville, it came directly from my complicated heart.

In Rockville, meanwhile, support for the lorises was withdrawn by degrees. It was a gentle process. Manners are not lacking in our town. But all the same. The city began a public-service campaign, a series of posters and radio ads entreating people to stop feeding the lorises, to reverse course on this trend. The admonishment: Don't ask, don't listen, don't feed. I saw a group of third-graders hustled past a murmuring, smiling loris lazily couchant on a branch above their heads, looking for all the world like Shere Khan or a serpent of Eden revised and softened to loosen the weakest joints in the soul of a child. They looked back over their shoulders with longing as she melted up into the tree.

One evening around this time I arrived home to a phone call from my friend the chef. She had made a discovery. It seemed that the oil of the loris, the fat left behind in the pan, could be sprinkled with gray sea salt and

poured over a salad of leafy greens to delicious effect. My friend had tried this first with spinach, and then with a few nontraditional greens as well—poke salad and burdock and thistle. Inspired by the results, she had been experimenting with the juice, creating sauces and glazes and dressings for all kinds of things, from pork chops to snakehead fillets. The meat of the loris had yet to give up any worthwhile secrets, but its oily drippings, evidently, made other foods good.

I was pleased. I cautioned my friend to take care not to poison herself by accident, and then I hung up the phone and sat down to consider the implications of this. Her discovery was well timed: new things were happening now, things that threatened to push the delicate relationship between lorises and Rockvillians from the lovely to the questionable to the ugly and unpleasant.

They were getting bossy and snarky. They were providing children with information about certain life processes before their parents deemed them old enough to hear this kind of news. They were telling people what to do more directly now, and people didn't like that. Some truths are more palatable than others.

Most disturbingly, a loris had followed a troubled young man out of the park and down a back street in the middle of the night. The young man quickened his step, but the loris maintained pursuit, warning the man furiously back from the wayward path his life had taken. The warnings became snarls, the man was cornered. When he tried to defend himself from further imploring, clamorous instructions, he was bitten savagely on his raised arms and face. The bossy loris was still at large, and the young man, though in stable condition, had provoked a rumble of public concern. What if dogs were eaten? What if children were harassed or misled? By this time the lorises had strayed far from the park and were sometimes sleeping under cars. It had become difficult to drive to work in the morning without the risk of running right over them. I decided I would visit my friend at her restaurant that very weekend to sample the results of her work.

When I joined her in the kitchen on Sunday morning, she had already arranged some items on a breakfast plate for me. What looked like ordinary pancakes and sausage were, as she explained, all products of invasive species. Every ground grain and berry had an unwelcome, ravenous origin, as did the sausage meat.

But instead of tasting like invasive species tend to taste—grasping, sinewy, caustic—they were sweet and mild. Every bite was delicious, including the pancakes, which were golden and knowable, despite containing some percentage of a dried ground caterpillar with no previous business in this biosphere. And it was all because of the loris oil. Everything had been touched by it and thus everything had been made good.

I told my friend she was a genius. She said she had me to thank, and then she made me an offer. She wanted to turn the restaurant into a trendy café, and she wanted me to co-own it with her. It would be called the World in Balance Café, and every night the special would be something plucked from a wilderness marred by its presence. We shook hands and it was done.

Night had fallen by the time we had worked out the details and I had driven home. As I dug in my purse for the keys to my front door, I heard a whispering in the shrubbery.

I stood very still. Despite the public-service announcements, I listened. I always listened.

Eight years have gone by now and after a successful run, the World in Balance is about to close. My chef friend and I are selling it to a vegan woman and her business partner who plan to transform it into a sushi bar with experimental live music performances on Tuesdays and Saturdays.

The lorises are almost gone—for the last few years we've leaned heavily on creative substitutions (truffle oil, chicken fat, mostly innocent alchemy). And I am a moderately wealthy woman, for the time being at least. In another five years, who can say where I'll be? I have this love situation, you see, and since love is as curious as any of the world's goods, I find myself at the dawn of another series of not entirely predictable events.

But in all this returning and returning, this washing machine of days in which each slosh is the jolt of a morning or a night, a sudden change, a swerve, a reversal, I somehow know when not to panic. I always seem to know.

It's Tuesday. It's snowing. I have had houseguests for the last few days. Now they have gone home, and I am gathering the wine glasses and thinking about all we have discussed, alone again with the sound of my own roaring blood. I'm older now, and nobody tells me what to do; that season has passed. But nothing else has changed.

Only this: I cannot afford to worry about a thing in this life. I'm telling you this. Not one thing, not even for a minute.

Kosciuszko

PETER ORNER

Barkus and I used to buy dope in Humboldt Park, beneath the giant equestrian statue of Thaddeus Kosciuszko. Our supplier was a woman who pretended to sell balloons. Well she did sell balloons. She just made more money off dope. I don't know where Barkus is now. I don't even know if he's alive. I only know that back then we used to buy the dope and smoke most of it right there in the car as we drove back to the suburbs, and Barkus would put his fist in his mouth and say in his pilot voice that *Pan Am flight whatever whatever whatever is cleared for landing. Roger that? Roger. Hey what happens when one of those guys really is named Roger? Or, shit, what about both of them? What happens when you've got two Rogers rogering each other? Roger, Roger. And a Roger Roger to you too, Roger. Sincerely yours, Roger.* Then we'd hit my driveway at forty miles an hour and nearly go through the garage.

Thaddeus Kosciuszko was a great Polish hero of the American Revolution. George Washington called him our Rock of Gibraltar. Had it not been for Kosciuszko the redcoats would have overrun the fort at West Point and we'd all to this day say *aubergine*. Thank you, Kosciuszko. I'm sure we disrespected your memory by buying dope beneath your horse's raised left hoof, but considering that you and your deeds are largely forgotten by those who should remain forever grateful, maybe the fact that I repeat your name—Kosciuszko!—keeps you less dead a little longer.

The balloon lady? I hope she got rich and retired. She was abrupt with a customer—the transaction had to be done fast. You had to have exact change. And you also had to buy a balloon, a couple of balloons if you wanted to endear yourself to her. She was of unfathomable age, not so old maybe but very wrinkled. She wore clown makeup and baggy pants with bells up and down the legs. Tall red boots. You could find her under Kosciuszko on Tuesday through Friday. She liked a three-day weekend. She kept her dime bags neatly done up in Ziplocs. Homegrown, Mexican-grown, Costa Rican–grown. Panamanian Special. The balloon lady was a clown, but her face never contorted into anything other than the one frozen smile, which was nothing at all like a smile. The clown was all business. If she had to wear that getup to make a living she had to wear that getup. The cops must have known all about her. They must have looked the other way. Or maybe they too were customers. Barkus once said the balloon lady was an artist, that the outfit, the unsmiling smile, the bells, the boots—all of it was a performance and another proof that what makes Chicago truly great is its people. Jane Addams, Mr. Sears and Mr. Roebuck (aka Mr. Rosenwald), Paddy Bauler, Mayor Daley, Floyd Kalber, Walter Payton, Roland Harper, Ivan DeJesus, Steve Ontiveros, Steve Dahl, the balloon lady. Barkus would say things like this, things that at first were stupid; then if you thought about them for a while they were still stupid, but less so, which is something given how many stupid things stay stupid. She could have just sold drugs. She didn't have to go through all the trouble. And think about it, every day she had to fill those balloons with helium. After a while even helium's not that fun anymore. "Why?" Barkus said. "Why does she do it? Because it's artful. This is what an artist does. Artists make work for themselves for absolutely no reason at all."

See? Barkus is nowhere I will ever see him again and still he's got me repeating his nonsense. It's been years since I've been as high as I was with Barkus. Once he took his hands off the wheel and shouted, "To home, gentle steed!" Edens Expressway, four in the morning. We scrawled across three lanes and were about to slam into the guardrail when I grabbed the wheel and righted us. There are many more near-misses I could tell you about and others I can only guess at. Have you found whatever you were looking for, Barkus? Peace? Artfulness? I imagine you by the side of some New Mexican highway, selling dreamcatchers and crystals. Is this too obvious? I guess this is the good imagining because there are days I am sure you

never made it, that you went flinging over that guardrail and down the embankment and so on. But maybe you needed me around to be really stupid and without me you moved on to blessed average. Now you sell life insurance in DeKalb. There's no one to ask. Your mother left town a year after you did.

Once—it must have been 1985—us in the car, the balloons bobbing against the roof, those dull thumps, and Barkus said, "I just got nostalgia for just now."

"What?"

"I'm missing this."

"Missing what?"

"This. Us driving. It's already gone. The Kennedy merges into the Edens. Next exit Peterson. Touhy, Dempster, Old Orchard, Tower Road… Bear right for 94 to Milwaukee. How come we never go to Milwaukee? Why doesn't anybody ever go to Milwaukee?" He stopped, leaned over, and drove a little while with his forehead. "But anyway it's gone," he said. "All of it. Even Milwaukee. Gone. Don't you miss it?"

"Dope's making speeches."

"Yes and no."

Here's the thing. Maybe I get it now. It is all gone. But the dangers have become more real and more dull without you. Kosciuszko was a hero. After he helped us win our revolution, he went back to Poland to start another one there. His rebellion lasted about twenty minutes. The Rock of Gibraltar shrunk to a pebble. The Russians were meaner motherfuckers than the British. They threw Kosciuszko in prison where he told some visiting prince that he regretted being alive, having so failed his country. Now there's a man. Chicago put up a statue of him in Humboldt Park. He rides a horse. He waves a sword. Chicago is full of such statues. Dr. Vardiman Black, the founder of modern dentistry. Friedrich Jahn who gave us gym class. I once got a blow job at the big bare feet of Goethe himself. Because real heroes once walked the earth and Chicago saluted them in stone. The rest of us are nostalgic pygmies.

Following a Lifetime of Fabrication.
In the Wake of Decades at Sea.

JOHN THORSON

After years of pretending to search for a creature I'd imagined, I accidentally discovered it. My colleagues put aside their hate for me and we celebrated our good fortune with champagne and Red Bull. My God, we all said, What a relief.

Tensions between my crew and I had been simmering in the weeks leading up to the capture thanks to a series of unlucky foul-ups that had called my authority into question, the most recent occurring one day prior, when we were radioed and told to pack up, our funding had been withdrawn and no one was going to be paid. After that most of the science team refused to look me in the eye, and those that still looked, that's all they did, and they refused to quit looking, even when I asked them to stop. But twenty-four hours later all was forgotten. We spent the night drunkenly dancing in circles around our captive. The mindfish looked so sad and beautiful in its holding tank, illuminated by strobe light. I felt like riding it.

The next morning the sunrise was brilliant. There were no clouds. The sky reflected off the ocean and everything was pink followed by fuchsia followed by yellow followed by blue. I'd stayed up to keep the mindfish company and was probably still wasted, but the science team had a hangover so I volunteered to make breakfast. I used the last of the waffles. Everyone had seconds. I fed the leftovers to the mindfish.

Reporters and photojournalists were lined up waiting for us when we docked. We took turns waving from the prow until a woman wearing our company's uniform came aboard. She asked which one of us was me and I told her I was. She smiled and took me by the hand and guided me off the ship, through the crowd and across the tangled cords of an impressive PA system, to a podium where a man I didn't recognize was in the middle of introducing me. And here he is, the man said. He turned toward me and opened his arms in a wide pre-hug gesture, and I stepped into full view and embraced him. The crowd cheered, and the man pulled me in further, so that his mouth was right next to my ear. "We will be very unhappy if this turns out to be another puppet," he whispered. Then he let me go, and I turned to face my waiting audience.

"The mindfish is real," I announced over the loudspeaker. The applause was deafening.

That night the mindfish and I attended a gala held in our honor. I wore a company tuxedo; the mindfish drifted within a golf cart filled with water, custom-converted for that purpose. Together we mingled with the world's scientific elite.

Years ago, when I began my expedition, had I thought ahead to its possible outcomes, I would never have imagined such an exquisite party. Men who had called me an insane con artist then, who had said that only a liar would claim that such a thing could exist, now shook my hand and asked me to pose with them in pictures. The mindfish loved it. Eventually we were asked to speak. I read a short something I had written in the limousine earlier that evening. The mindfish decided to wing it and delivered an impromptu speech that was humble and genuine and iambic and rhymed entirely. The room leapt to its feet and cheered and surged and shouted, "We love you too, mindfish." Spotlights were shining on both of us. I climbed the mindfish's golf cart and raised both my arms like an Olympic gold medalist. Indoor fireworks exploded overhead.

An hour of vodka drinks later, the mindfish and I found ourselves wedged into a semicircle booth packed with VIPs and glitterati. Everyone at the table was sharing their favorite cocaine stories. The biochemist to my left was showing us how he'd done lines off a rotating subway turnstile when I felt a hand clasp my shoulder. It was the man who'd introduced me at the podium. I offered him my gimlet.

"I'm glad you're having a good time," he said. He asked if I was right enough to talk business.

"I'm as right as a rainbow," I said. And I all of a sudden realized everyone else had left the table and the mindfish and I were now sitting alone. The man smiled.

"Good," he said, and stepped aside to reveal the person who had been standing behind him, whom I hadn't noticed until just then. It took five blinks to register the gold uniform and recognize my company's CEO.

"I'd like to shake your hand," said the CEO. "I'd really like to shake your hand."

I tried to stand, but the booth's cushions were too slick and everything was too glossy and there was vomit somewhere in my throat and all I could think about was vomit. I was filled with vomit and the CEO's golden uniform was hurting my eyes.

"He's doing this on purpose," I said.

I tried to get up a second time, but my brain tripped. I saw my older brother chasing me down a crowded supermarket aisle. I saw my father waving to me from the other side of an airport terminal. I saw my ex-wife changing for bed with her back turned, kicking off her jeans and unhooking her bra, and I wanted her to face me, I wanted to see her naked, but my brain tripped again and my head jerked upwards and I made eye contact with the mindfish. Its expression was a mother's heartbeat, comfort and concern, but in its eyes I saw my reflection. I saw my face about to vomit. I saw my eyes reflecting the mindfish's eyes, and in the mindfish's eyes I saw an intelligence containing so much infinity that for a moment it felt like it might forgive me for ever thinking I could have invented it.

A Record of Our Debts

LAURA HENDRIX

Selma's on the woodpile now. She's been out there all day; nobody knows what to do. Daddy says he knows what—"I sure as shit know what I'm gonna do with that girl soon as she gits her ass inside," he says. He says that but of course he doesn't, because if he did he'd go out there and get Selma and do it. But she's just sitting up there on top of the logs which aren't even split yet and guess what she's doing. *She's eating the wood.* Legs all splayed, kicking, swinging. She's picking long splinters off the ends of logs, then breaking them up into smaller splinters, little mulch pile in the lap of her dress. She'll take a few of the splinters, put them in her mouth, and chew. I got right up close and watched her for a time. She stared straight past me like I wasn't even there. Teeth grinding, shiny wet lips, and her dark little mouth chewing hard, trying to make enough juice to break up all that wood, which you are *not even supposed to eat.* Good god jesus christ almighty.

Selma's not the only one who's sick. But because she's pretty far gone, and started to go early on, noticeable-like, some people pretend it's only her. *Crazy Selma,* they'll say, and laugh. And then they'll go back to chewing the bloody skin around their fingernails, hoping nobody notices who else is sick right along with her.

She doesn't come back inside that day. Supper happens, sun goes down, Daddy lights a fire, him and Mama sit by it and talk a while, trying not to look outside. Then they go to bed. I wait on Selma, adding logs to the stove every once in a while. By the time she comes in it's deep night, and she's got the shivers so bad I have to put her by the fire and wrap my arms around her, her teeth chattering so hard they're like to break. "You hungry?" I ask her. She shakes her head. There's something funny in her look. Dropped eyes. She looks like she's been shamed by what she's done. This gives me hope, which I haven't had for Selma in quite some time.

* * *

The town is not what it used to be. Not that it ever was that much. A couple of stores, post office, schoolhouse, church. But still. Things here are going, as Daddy says, all to shit. Post office doesn't run every day anymore. Doesn't need to, with letters being mostly nonsense, addressed to the neighbor's mule, to God, to the fountain in the center of town. This is what I learned, in any case, from Lon Henry, the postmaster's son, who is like me not sick yet, and still able to notice such things.

Another thing different is nobody minds the store anymore. Sure, Mrs. Lemon still sits up there behind the counter, watches what you get, and writes something down in her little book, but she's stopped even asking for cash money on the spot, tells everybody they can pay later, whether they've got the money ready to offer her or not. The other day I went up there, did our shopping, and put down on the counter what we needed. Mrs. Lemon scribbled away, hardly even looking up at me. Her ledger should have said, *3 pounds flour, soap, 1 pound coffee*. But I looked at it. It said *charge, charged* and *you owe, you owe, you owe* and *who will pay what you owe*. I am frightened by this. Because if Mrs. Lemon is not, then who is keeping a record of our debts? And if there is no record of our debts, then what on earth might we be asked to pay?

Now, or perhaps before now, I should tell when it started, this illness. Because I am telling the story, and a story must have a place to start out from, a thing that happened to start the other things. And here is the problem. We simply do not know. Perhaps someone does. Perhaps someone did a thing one day, some horrible thing, and this brought the illness upon him or her, upon all of us. But if so, it was a thing done in secret, in the dark, and we have not uncovered it.

This morning, mother tells me to go into town again. What for? I ask, although I know what for, because I see Daddy holding Selma down on the bed and I know

NEPALIKIME MIŠKE !
DEGANČIO LAUŽO !

that she's in one of her fits. Blood fits, we call them, because she bites and scratches, not just herself but us too. The thought occurs to me that my mother believes that there are still certain harms that she can protect me from.

It's a short walk, not a quarter mile, but with no other reason to move about, I am grateful for it. It is comforting to have a goal, a reason to put one foot in front of the other. When I get there, I see Lon Henry sitting out in the gazebo by the fountain. Sun's hot, so I go and join him in the shade.

"Hey," I say.

He nods.

"What're you doing?"

He shrugs. "Waiting, I guess."

"What for?"

Lon shrugs again. "Something to happen."

"Why aren't you at the post office?"

"Didn't feel like it. There was a bunch of folks hanging around there this morning, talking crazy. How's Selma?"

"Not so good."

"They talk about her, you know. All them crazies. Even Daddy. They think she's the reason."

"Yeah, I know." I've heard them talk. "But she ain't."

"I know it."

Because neither of us has a thing in the world to do, we decide to go to Mrs. Lemon's store and get some licorice. We pause for a moment in our negotiating, remembering that neither of us has any money, and then remembering that not having any money doesn't matter, not anymore, not at Mrs. Lemon's store.

Lon shuffles his feet as we walk. I have always admired his gait, and though to some it might make him look ill or lame, I love the look of it, the lines his toe drags in the dusty road, so that when we walk together and I look behind us I can see the proof of where we have been.

We get to the store and it looks a shambles. Looks like somebody let a gang of raccoons loose in there—bins turned over, floor covered with gummy beans and

PASTEBĖJĘ GAISRĄ MIŠKE,
PRANEŠKITE GIRININKIJAI.

mashed-up crackers. Mrs. Lemon sits on the floor in the middle of it all, feet bare, her skirt hiked up to reveal swollen white knees. Behind her stands Lon's father. He's trying to hold her head still, and she's pulling against him, writhing like a cat. Her face is dirty, smeared with a crust of flour and snot. She's laughing like a maniac.

"You," she shrieks, and Mr. Henry says it at the same time. "What do you mean coming here?" he says to me. "Ain't your family done enough?"

Mrs. Lemon is laughing still, but now I notice there are tears running through her furrowed face. "Enough, enough!" she says. "There's not enough. Store's closed on account of not enough." Her head sets to moving again, trying to bang against a wall that isn't there.

"My family?" I say to him. "What's my family ever done to you?"

Lon's daddy spits right onto the floor. "What ain't they done? Not just to me. To all of us. You tell her, Lon." He's about to be yelling. Lon just shakes his head, though, and looks at the floor, all the waste.

"Come back tomorrow," says Mrs. Lemon. "We'll get more. We'll get it back."

"Go on, then!" Mr. Henry shouts at me. "You get home, girl, and stay the hell away from my boy."

Mrs. Lemon is still laughing and crying and promising, and so we walk out of that store in reverse, scared to turn our backs on them. In front of us, of course, on the wooden floorboards, Lon's shuffle doesn't leave any mark.

Once outside, we don't even talk about what happened in there. It just sticks like a lump in each of our throats, indigestible, unspeakable. Lon and I walk together for a few steps, and then part.

"Bye," I tell him. He nods.

It's nearly dark by the time I get home. Selma's worn herself out. She's passed out cold on the floor, and for some reason Mama and Daddy have just left her there.

"Aren't you going to put her in the bed?" I ask.

Mama laughs, an exhausted, desperate kind of laugh. "What for?" she says. "She'll just wake up tomorrow and get back out of it." She laughs some more. Daddy does not seem to think this is funny either. We share a glance, and somewhere in his eye, I accidentally recognize a splinter of fear. And at that moment I know something that I truly wish I did not, because if I didn't know, maybe I could get to sleep tonight without thinking, over and over, *Well good goddamn, Mama's going, too.*

Selma's having a good day when she gets up. It isn't until noon that she wakes, but she rises with a washed calm on her face, all the confusion spent. She's a pond left still after a rain, a wolf sauntering away when the feast is done.

"Take me into town," she says to me.

I think about what Mr. Henry said. "Town's no good, Selma."

"How come?"

"People are sick there."

"I'm sick," she says to me in a low voice.

"How do you know that?"

She leans in and whispers in my ear. "I *feel* different." Instead of leaning away, she drops her head onto my shoulder and lets it rest there, her eyes closed. When we were small, playing near the creek, she would sit by me that way.

I kiss her head. I figure, if we see him, we can just cross the street. "Okay, Sellie," I tell her. "Let's go into town."

Daddy joins us. Mama's been picking at him all morning about things he can't make sense of—why he never replaced our mule that died two years ago; how sun is so much hotter this year—and he wants to get away.

He tries to speak to us some on the way into town. Daddy is a quiet man, except when he's angry, and it's rare that he tries to be conversational. "Girls, look at these tracks," he says. "Looks like the boars were through here this morning."

We both nod, unable to think of a response. This is not news. The boars come through every morning.

"And girls," he says, bending over to examine a line of ants. "Look down here. Closer." We three crouch, the line of ants weaving between us. They are carting away their dead. One of the ants, unmoving, rests upturned on the back of another, and the other ants follow.

"How come they do that, Daddy?" I ask. "Is it like a funeral?"

"Nobody knows. What do you think?"

"I think maybe they don't want to leave the other ant behind," I say. "Maybe he's important."

Selma chews on her thumb for a moment, her head cocked. "That ain't it," she huffs, spitting out a bit of fingernail. "They're taking his body home, so's the rest of them can eat it."

Daddy stares at her.

I don't say so, but I was just trying to be pleasant before. Of course they're going to eat it.

Once in town, we don't know what to do. There is no church today, and we are not a town with a picture show. We walk through slowly, taking in the damage. People sit on porches in twos and threes but talk to themselves if they talk at all. Hungry dogs roam around, eyes agleam. No one's burned garbage in some time, it seems, because there's a stink, and crows swarming the piles like messes of flies.

"Hey there," someone calls out from a porch. The man is not looking at us; his gaze squirms toward the heavens. "Hey," he says again, louder this time. "Is that her? Is that that Selma?"

Daddy puffs up. On instinct, he steps in front of his smallest girl. "What's your business?" he says to the man, who thinks on this for a while.

"I want things back like they was," he says. "I want my home and my wife back. I want your girl to pay for this curse she's brought down upon us."

"My Selma ain't done nothing to you."

"Sure she done. Look around, son. Look what's become of this town since you been bringing your crazy, sick daughter into it. She's cursed. She's cursed us all."

SAUGOKIME
IŠKUS NUO GAISRU

Daddy starts to walk, tries to take Selma's hand and lead her off and away from this. But she goes still behind him, and so we have to, too. Breath and blinking and heartbeats suspended. We wait to see what will happen. Selma turns her face toward the dead-eyed old man. She grins. And then she lunges. Suddenly she is a whirlwind. Daddy holds on, tries to still her and can't. Selma's eyes are slits on fire, her mouth an ugly tear with bared teeth and wild tongue pushing through. She lets out an animal scream, a growl, the awful sounds of a thing trying to kill another thing. Her face also speaks. *You do not know cursed*, it says. *You do not know it now, but you will.* All the time she is hitting, twisting, trying to get at him. I duck down beneath her and she bloodies my eyes but I can still see her. I see what this man sees.

Daddy is able at last to pin her arms. He picks Selma up onto his hip and she goes slack, empty. She's light enough for him to carry, all skin and bones, but too tall to be held like a baby. Her long limp legs nearly drag on the ground as he hauls her, with me following, back toward home.

That night, dinner is plucked chicken served half-raw on a plate. Mama sits by and laughs. The rest of us all eat it. Don't hardly even notice.

Later, Daddy comes into mine and Selma's room and he shakes me awake. I start to groan, trying to form a question, but he puts a finger to his lips so I get quiet. We walk out into the big room.

"What is it?" I ask.

"I don't like to say this to you. I don't. But we need to be watching Selma pretty close for a while."

"What do you mean?"

"I mean don't let her go off anywheres. Don't let her get out of your sight."

"Okay." I don't have to ask the reason.

There is a long silence and Daddy scratches his head and looks down into his lap. "I'm sorry I have to put this on you," he says.

And I'm sorry too. God, am I sorry. I don't want to be the one my father wakes in the night with his troubles.

The sound begins the next morning before the sun. I hear a rhythm, a pulsing, and it draws me from my dream into waking. At first I think that it is my own heart-beat, but it goes on outside of me, steady and strong, so unlike the raggedy fearful ticking in my chest.

I reach out for Selma in the space beside me. "What's that sound?" I ask her.

"Probably they're coming to get me," she says. "Boo! Boo!" She giggles, rolls over, and goes back to sleep. Her tiny body rises and falls beside me.

The men arrive that morning, wearing funeral clothes and lunatic grins. They are haggard. Frayed at the edges. There are six of them lined up in two columns. I can still hear that sound, carried in on the morning wind from town. A pulse of voices, a song or chant, a prayer, I cannot tell which. But the men stomp in time to it, not needing to hear it clearly, knowing it in their hearts already, their heavy boots pounding the dust of our yard with almost spiteful force. Daddy goes to the door and I peek out from behind him. He tries to push me back but I don't go.

The first one steps forward. From the others, there is a low hum, an echo of the noise from town. Pulse, beat. "Bring out the girl," the first one says. There is a fren-zied gleam in his eyes. Perhaps it is why he was selected for this task, or volunteered.

"You ain't taking her," Daddy says.

The man spits onto the ground. "Figure we will. We got to."

Daddy lifts a shotgun from his side and points it at the men, and this is when I notice then that they themselves are not armed. The knowledge sinks me. These men are wild past fearing guns, or needing them. Daddy's still aiming on the one in the front, but they don't even see any gun.

Most of them, anyway. One does. There's Lon Henry, his small head sticking out from the back of the line. He shuffles to the front, between them and us, just a few feet from my father's gun, then looks away from us and back at the men. He still has the decency for that.

"Let's go," he says to them, waving them back with his arms. "It ain't no good. Let's get on out of here."

They shrug and grumble, unsure. But then they turn to go. He is a boy, Lon, no more than eleven, no more than four feet tall, and with a gimp leg. I wonder if these men are so lost they would follow anyone who stood up in front of them.

"Wait for us," the one who spoke first says as they go. "We'll be back." Lon turns and looks at me then, already sorry, and I know he'll be with them. They all turn and walk away, in time with each other, in time with the sound. From the window Selma watches them and tries to hum along.

Afterward we sit around the kitchen table. All four of us, like a family, though but for that it doesn't seem it. We are four people, each of us walled up. Mama has glazed eyes and chews her lip. Daddy swills from a jar of liquor. Selma beats out that awful rhythm on the table with her raw knuckles, and I try to understand what has happened to all of us. The noise gets to Daddy. "Goddamnit, Selma, quit that. I can't hear my own thoughts."

"What's to think about, Daddy?" She looks up at him. "Somebody's got to pay."

"Well, it ain't gonna be us."

Selma shrugs. "I reckon it will be."

"It won't," he insists.

But Mama seems not to have heard him. She nods. "Yes. Somebody's got to pay."

That night I wake up and find Selma gone. I jump out of bed running for the door, thinking what to grab, but she is there in the main room. She is taking sticks from the kindling pile and tying them together with floss, in the shape of little bodies. She plays with the bodies not as a girl does, but as a baby would. She puts them in her mouth, sucks on them, grows weary of them, stomps on them or smashes them up with her fists.

Daddy is sitting there too, staring at her. His eyes

are blank, and I am sure that he doesn't even know what he's looking at anymore. I believe it is at this moment that he begins to agree.

They come to us again the next day, in greater numbers. There is still the rhythm, and each of them contributing to it. They stomp, and beat the ground with sticks, and slap at their own legs and shoulders, and grind their teeth. Some of them sing, hymns that once I recognized but feel now I am hearing for the first time. We wait inside all day, but they do not go away that night. Rather, they keep on coming, more and more of them, until we are sure the whole town has come to the woods. It has brought its people and its tools and all of its sickness along with it, and now it lives here with us.

It's a blood red sun the next morning, and the moon still raised on the other side of the sky. We have not slept, nor have the visitors. I can only think we are half delirious with the pounding noise and exhaustion. Otherwise I can't explain why it is that I follow Mama and Daddy, with little Selma swinging like a paper doll between them, into the yard.

My only hope at that moment is that the noise will stop. That they will all be stilled, there will be quiet, and it will be finished. Which is not what happens. Instead, it grows louder. Chants turn to shouts, yells so loud that I swear to God they are ripping their throats on the sound. I can hear the blood rattling in the hollows. There is no kind of order here. No representative to step forward and take our offering, no ceremony in place. They rush for us all at once. A herd of men and women, their fury unrestrained, with hair in their eyes and blood on their teeth. They take our baby Selma. They take her and they tear her apart.

And it does not get better, after all.

History Lesson

NELLY REIFLER

KAŽDÝ TÝDEN

ÚZV - Praha 70 - Solo Lipník ČSN - 49 4705

He pried the log open. Half-rotted, it split easily. It gave off a spray of moldy dust along the break. She coughed and covered her mouth and nose with her hair. Her throat, already parched and tight, contracted. He fanned the air in front of his face with his hand.

They both stepped forward and examined the inside of the log. Centipedes wriggled along channels in the disintegrating wood. A few fat white grubs lolled in the damp end.

"Well?" she said. In parts of the world people lived on such things.

They had been lost for over a day. They had spent the night shivering on a rocky hill. It had been very cold up there on the ridge, but together they had come to the conclusion that it was better there than in the swampy lowlands with their blood-thirsty insects and encroaching spores. When I say *together*, I mean that they had negotiated, each being no more of an expert than the other. When I say *conclusion* I refer to a point at which the one upon whose shoulders had fallen the task of arguing in favor of the lowlands conceded to the ridge defender with a certain sense of relief. She had been on the lowlands side, and she'd been sure that he was wrong about the ridge. He was always wrong, but she always wanted him to be right. And so she had conceded, and in this case it didn't matter. It rarely mattered. I do *love* him, she was known to say.

She crouched down to pick up a grub. She just barely touched the cluster of faintly segmented white bodies, and they dispersed instantly. They had looked so slow and lazy. Now they were gone.

Meanwhile, he had found a long stick. He remembered seeing a documentary in which indigenous people lowered a stick into a rotten log and the insects they desired for roasting and eating clamored up it. As he lowered his own stick, he talked to himself inside his head. He told himself not to scold, mock, or punish her in any way for so clumsily—fucking idiotically—scaring away the grubs. He would remain silent.

If she asked, he would say he wasn't angry.

He poked the end of the stick into the center of a channel where centipedes slithered. They ignored his stick, going right around it as if it were nothing, nothing but a stick. He felt his face heat up. He threw the stick on the ground and stamped on it with his boot.

"It was a good idea," she said. "Don't be hard on yourself. Maybe there's something in the other half of the log. Something sluggish, like a slug."

"I don't think slugs live in logs," he said.

"They do," she said. "Banana slugs." She had no idea what she was talking about.

The larger, heavier piece of the log had tumbled into a shallow puddle a few feet away when he'd split it. He stepped on the useless stick to hear it crack once more, then kicked it, then stepped over to the puddle.

She only noticed him staggering backward out of the corner of her eye. She had been thinking that she was right all along about hiking in the autumn. She was playing with sentences in her head, things she might say if she were the type to tell him he was wrong. Which she was not. But if she were, she would remind him that she had specifically said that it's harder to find paths when they're covered with fallen leaves, and that the only edible things left in the forest this time of year are wild onions, if you're lucky, and those don't provide you with much nourishment. Would she bring up the ridge? Surely, the aridity of the ridge had dehydrated them more than the moisture of the lowlands would have sickened them.

Often when you feel terribly hungry, what you're really experiencing is severe dehydration. Hunger takes much longer than thirst to become dangerous.

He staggered backward. He looked over at her, and she was gazing at nothing, eyes narrowed, frowning, shaking her head back and forth, licking her lips. He clasped her by both shoulders and pulled her up. He didn't say anything, just dragged her over to the second piece of log. And there we were.

"What…" Her voice choked a little, and she grabbed his hand.

"You see them, too, right?" he said.

"I don't know. What do *you* see?"

He squatted and reached a single finger out.

"Don't touch them!" she cried.

"That's okay," I said, sighing. "You can touch."

KAŽDÝ DEN

He looked up at her. I looked at her, too. Her eyes were very dark and wet.

"It said it's okay," he said.

I looked at us through their four eyes.

In the moist hollow of the log, our heads were pressed together; my ear pushed into your cheek. My chin was at your temple. Our legs were tucked up with our knees at our bellies. Our toes pointed in opposite directions. Our arms stretched over our heads, and our little fingers interlaced. Our faces were chubby enough, but our ribs showed in a way that made them both frightened.

"Don't be frightened," I said.

"You do it," he said to her. "Touch."

"I think we should go," she said. She tried to figure out what he was thinking, and told herself to be the voice of reason.

I started crying. You trembled a little next to me, but made not a sound. My tears were hot and wetter than regular water. I had never cried before. I pitied both of them as I cried; I had never felt pity before.

"Don't leave us," I sobbed.

"We won't," he said, reaching toward us again and thinking that maybe they would leave us or maybe not. He very slowly crossed the final sliver of air between his fingers and my skin. I could feel the approach of his thumb, its frequency, the molecules vibrating. Cells dislodged and flaked off into the atmosphere as he stroked my arm with the thumb. I found that the action slowed my sobbing, and finally the tears stopped coming, too.

"It's so soft," he said. "The skin is so soft."

"Let's go," she said. "They must be someone's. It can't be our responsibility."

"How could they be someone's? All the way out here? And look at the way the wood has grown around them—those knots? That's what's holding them in there."

Already she had been thinking about how their lives had become too intertwined. She had been too accommodating. How could she have done that with someone who was always wrong?

I could feel you shuddering next to me; you didn't understand what was happening. You flickered: moment

to moment you were in this world or the other. Your thoughts were shadows, angles, dots muddling around each other attempting to form colors. I feared for you.

"Don't leave us," I said again. The crying had thickened my voice. "We're hungry, too. Look at these ribs! I can show you the way out of here, and then none of us will be hungry or thirsty anymore."

She squinted and shook her head. It's not that she was without tenderness. It was that she was at this point knowledgeable in the ways of tenderness, how it can lead to sacrifices and stretches of time given over to futile activities; in a finite life, stretches of time mean something.

He possessed less native tenderness, but strove for valiance as a kind of cantilever to a life which had not yet amounted to much.

"I think we should take them," he said. "It would be…"—he thought about a way to translate it into her language—"downright immoral to leave them here. Besides, if it's telling the truth, we need its help as much as it needs ours."

She sighed, conceding once again. Concessions carried their own pure satisfaction, she supposed.

With his penknife, he worked on the wood that indented our flesh, and he sliced the small shriveled vines that connected the centers of our abdomens to the log's dry pulp. He carried me, she carried you. I directed them back to the path from which they had strayed the previous morning, and reminded them to turn at the blue spray-paint arrows, not the orange ones. Their automobile was exactly as they had left it in the parking lot, under the shade of the oak, nose in the honeysuckles, near the wooden garbage station. She did not admit to herself, until she saw the car, how convinced she had become that they would never leave the forest.

From the beige velour of the back seat where we lay, I peered through the glass and watched the trees blur. I nearly lost hold of the idea that we were the ones moving through space, and that the trees were standing still.

In this world, glue is often made from the hard parts of dead animals.

In this world, things happen, and then other things

PŘED KAŽDÝM JÍDLE

follow. Think of it like this: there is a line, and on that line there are different lengths demarcated by numbers in sequence. Time, you see, is this line. The first number is us, there, in the log, in the forest. The second number, just a bit further along the line, is the apartment on that street in the city. Now imagine a longer stretch, further still, and here we find ourselves in the place in the shade near the road. Do you see how it works? It's a common metaphor. I'm not partial to metaphors, but sometimes they're the only solution.

I suppose that if you could argue, you might argue that the line should stretch in the other direction, as well, into the realm of negative numerals. Do you by any chance remember the plasma? The jelly before we had skin? I'd put that era somewhere around negative two on the line. Zero would be all xylem and phloem.

Related to this way of looking at time, I'll explain something that they had in common: they were both wanters. They traveled along the line with a steady pulse of yearning. The thing about wanters is that, since desire is constant, so is dissatisfaction. If you are this way, you may grasp precisely the thing for which you yearned and inevitably it does not change the way your nervous system works. That itch continues—it just moves to another part of your flesh.

One of her complaints about him was that he always wanted to fix things; she was correct. During our second week in the apartment, when we were starting to become mobile, he noticed how gingerly you pulled yourself along the floor. I had decided not to mention to them the aggressive hardness of the oak planks and its bruising effect on my limbs and digits. You didn't know better, and you whimpered and sucked on your sore, reddened palms. He left the apartment and came back an hour later with a big bolt of something gray. He picked us each up under one arm and placed us on their bed, which was covered in a large cotton sack filled with the tiny belly feathers of geese. How soft it was. You sank backward into it and closed your eyes, rocking slightly. I heard furniture being moved around in the living room, and a little later some banging noises. The apartment was always noisy, pervaded by the racket from four stories below: trucks barreling or idling, car alarms, beasts tied up and crying for their masters. It was unusual for the sounds inside to rise above those from outside.

KAŽDÝ DEN ČISTÉ

When he returned to the bedroom, he sat down between us.

"This comforter is very soft," I said.

"You know she won't let you sleep here," he said. "But hopefully I've made an improvement."

When she came back from her daily round of errands, she stopped short in the doorway. She wanted to yell at him; she wanted to throw her new bottle of shampoo at his head. Instead she made herself smile as she stepped into the apartment and placed her plastic sacks down on the table. "Sweetie," she said, "you know how I feel about carpeting."

"They were hurting," he said. "They were bruising."

I tried my best to twinkle up at her from the gray synthetic surface. Its underlying layer of foam rubber added a pleasant cushion.

"I just tacked it in the corners with a few nails," he said. "It doesn't have to be permanent."

Something had altered since they found us in the woods: the simple act of cutting us out of the log had made him giddy with its suggestion of how easy it is to shift, and awestruck by how shifting one thing can make everything else feel new. As if life were endless, which in this story it is not.

She sighed and carried her shampoo into the bathroom.

More than anything, he *wanted* "things" to "change," and once during our time in that apartment I heard him say, pointing to us, "They represent change." Were you a theoretically minded reader, little one, you might want to correct him. *No*, you'd say to him, pointing at us, *we represent the two of you: you and her*. But you would be wrong, too. You and I are certainly not mere metaphors.

He made us toys: one day he sanded down chunks of pine into building blocks and painted them yellow and blue. Another day he mixed food coloring with flour, water, and salt. He started buying us things: one week he bought me a kazoo and you a small plastic mallet that chirped when it hit something hard. The next week he hung a barometer outside of one window, and outside

of the other he hung a thermometer; he announced that we would enjoy learning about the weather. She went about her business; all of her interaction with us was quiet and still. She needed to "focus."

Were you a reader who had expectations, you might expect to find fault with one or the other, to designate a hero and a villain; in this world the tendency to pick sides is ingrown, evolutionarily determined.

From our stations on the floor, we were unable to see either of the meteorological instruments.

The conversations in that small apartment often went like this: she would be sitting at their table staring at a screen, her face illuminated by the glow of light passed through polarizing filters and heliacal liquid crystal. He would start pacing first, glancing at us, then at her. Usually, although she appeared to be concentrating fiercely on her work, her mind was jittering, bouncing from her regrets to her grandiose ambitions. Usually, although he *seemed* to be animated by some powerful male force, he was, inside himself, talking himself out of his timidity and gearing up to present her with an idea about *change* and how things needed to.

Sometimes he would say: "We should move to the country. That's where we found them. The urban life isn't good for them."

And she would say: "I'm almost finished with this. Can it wait?"

And I would contribute: "She really needs to finish her project."

Other times he would say: "I'm thinking of taking some kind of class for them, like puppet-making or book-binding or psychodrama."

And she would say: "That sounds good."

And he would say: "Do you want to take it with me?"

And she would say nothing.

And I would proffer: "You can read about book-binding online."

She told herself that we were a useful distraction for him; out of the corner of her eye she'd catch him making monkey noises for my entertainment or spelling out words on the refrigerator with magnetic letters. She wanted to be amused and charmed by this behavior, by all his new enthusiasms. But when she tried to smile, she felt her lips form a kind of grimace.

Early on in their courtship, he had made monkey noises for her. When they first took occupancy of the apartment he would spell out words on the refrigerator for her. No longer.

Some events truly are unexpected; surprise is a kind of mutation. Surprise, like copulation, is a phenomenon that only means something in a world such as this. Mistakes are the same as surprises—using one word or the other depends on a mood of blame or wonder. What happened next was that I made a mistake, and they surprised me.

One night in the apartment we were at our usual stations. He was pacing. She was at her screen. I was playing with a ball he had bought from a wire bin at a pharmacy; I'd been watching how the angles of its decorative diamond shapes became more obtuse when it rolled. The faster it rolled, the more obtuse the diamonds. I knew that this was a trick my eyes were playing, and that it had to do with the speed of light and my own rods and cones. You were sitting in a corner, forehead propped against the wall, foot in your mouth. I had grown since the log. You did not grow, and if you learned at all, it was at such a slow pace they could not see it. Here's one other thing they shared: they both felt ashamed of their discomfort with you. Their inability to attach warm feelings to you made them both feel shallow, as if they were the kind of people they despised. They saw you as a kind of appendage of me. When you shuddered and convulsed, he would— through a great act of will—pick you up and perform the routine of comforting.

VEČER A RÁNO

But he held, in his heart's black capsule, the belief that you were a wrong in this world. She tended to leave you alone. As a girl she had always felt a particular embarrassment on *behalf* of her grandmother's cocker spaniel with gummy eyes; that was how she felt about you, too.

This time the conversation started out as usual.

"Things need to change," he said. "We can't go on living in this stagnation, this limbo."

"I'm busy with my work," she said. "When I'm done with my project, maybe we can talk about it. Maybe things *will* change when I'm in a different place with my project."

He stopped in front of her. He took her chin in his hand and tilted her face toward his. "It's about sex," he said. He closed her screen. It clicked shut against the keyboard.

"I know," she said.

"I miss it," he said.

They looked at each other for a few seconds.

Leaning against the ball and smiling my most winning smile, I said, "Let her finish her project. Talk later about sex."

He sighed. She opened her screen, and it sang its little tune. I was quite proud of myself for maintaining things as they were. As much as he said we represented change, in truth my job was to make sure nothing changed. That's pretty easy when you're dealing with wanters. My mistake was believing that just because something is easy it is also permanent.

I winked at them, and then crawled over to you and whispered, "I am their glue."

It has been said that falling in love is like embarking on a voyage that nobody else has ever taken; if that is the case, then loving is like being on a boat nowhere near any shore. It might be said that one should be careful about falling in love, but also that one should pay no attention to that warning. If you haven't fallen in love yet, you don't know the brittle, drifting vessel that might end up conveying you when the time comes.

I might have forgotten about that particular conversation on that particular evening if you had not had your accident two days later. You had been placed on the dining-room table while some vacuuming was happening—they knew I would scurry away from the machine but didn't trust you not to get in the way. One of the table's leaves was wobbly, and as you lay there it flapped down under your weight. The leaf hit the table's base with a clatter that could be heard even over the machine's drone. At that very moment, he was going at the area under the table with the rug attachment. He tried to catch you as you fell. Lunging for you, though, he tripped over the vacuum's hose and

went flying himself. You landed on the carpet with a dull thud, and your body went rigid with shock. Your fists clenched and unclenched.

He knocked his head on the bookshelf and then crumpled, twisting his wrist and bending his thumb back when he tried to break his fall.

She saw the whole thing. It was *as if*, she would say later, *it was happening in slow motion*. She gasped and then screamed and dropped the mug she was washing. In spite of the chaos of the moment, it did not escape her notice that he had tried to catch you. At the thought of his sacrifice her eyes filled with fluid, and her chest ached in a way she'd believed had been lost. She ran over to him and cradled his head in her arms and helped him slowly rise. She made him sit down on the couch and brought him ice for his head and, for his wrist, a topical gel she had bought at the health-food store. I crawled across the carpet. While she tended to him, I tried to point out that you needed some ice and topical gel too. "Ahem," I said from where you'd fallen, near the table leg. "Over here." But there was no response. Their hearts were beating fast, and as I watched in horror they pressed their faces close to each other's and kissed in a way they had not kissed for years.

That night there was nothing I could do to stop them. Their genitals had become engorged. They started to peel off each other's clothes in front of us before they went into the bedroom and locked the door. I sat with my ear to the wood. The breaths and cries were unmistakable. I wanted to throttle you for being so careless, but punishment only matters if the one on the receiving end is capable of feeling guilt. Their thoughts were impenetrable from where I was. Probably they weren't thinking.

I waited gloomily for a week. Even when there was a fifth heartbeat in the apartment, I said nothing, hoping it would die before she noticed that anything had changed. But it didn't. It got stronger. Still I said nothing, hoping that they would not want to keep it. But now, looking back, I see that it makes perfect sense that they did.

She kept her secret from him until she was sure, until she knew that it had *taken*. That was the word she used inside her mind. When she was sure, she sat him down on the couch and gingerly took his hand (his injured thumb was still being kept rigid by a curved piece of blue fiberglass). I slunk into the darkest corner of the living room

and watched the scene unfold. She couldn't remember the last time she had been this nervous about telling him something. She hardly believed it herself, the thing she was about to say aloud. But she managed to do it: she announced her condition to him. After a few moments he began to laugh, and then he took her in his arms and inhaled the perfume of her hair.

She laughed with him. She knew then that she didn't really want to finish her project—in fact she'd been looking for something besides him upon which to blame its inevitable failure. And she was relieved that she no longer had to make a decision about how intertwined their lives were. He was glad, too: he could finally stop his pacing demands for change. Now *this* was change. His innate lack of tenderness, which had always nagged at him, suddenly felt compensated for by the new instinct he felt to protect her and the cells multiplying inside of her.

Over the next few months he continued to feed us, but no longer did he make us toys, no longer did he listen to my advice. I was stunned. I tried to start conversations with them, but they ignored me. It turns out that even if you know a lot, as I did, it doesn't mean you know everything. Even if you know everything at a given moment, it doesn't mean you'll know it when the moment changes.

Just about a year after they had been lost in the woods, they announced to us that we were going to take a ride in the country. By this point her belly had started to round over the waistband of her skirt, and her pelvic bones had begun to widen. They stood over us, united, with strange and glassy expressions. You were drooling and your eyes were closed. I sat there picking at my cuticles and frowning. Over time, I had become depressed and muddled; my faith had turned vaporous. Now I tried in vain to sense, through my haze, what their plan was.

They placed us in the back of the car with some of our favorite things. As we crossed the first bridge out of the city, I attempted once more to win them back. "Please," I said. "You're nothing without us. We need each other. I saved your life."

She sighed, and turned around in her seat. "The apartment is just too small for all of us," she said. I saw that her eyes were wet as she stroked my cheek. How rarely I had felt her skin against mine. It was so smooth and cool. "Besides, the urban life is probably not good for you."

"You're rationalizing," I said. She withdrew her hand and didn't say anything else.

They stopped at a rest stop where some willow trees had been planted near the dog run. I struggled as he lifted me out of the automobile, punching at his arm and biting at his shirt. You were confused but placid. They rested us under a willow, and she placed a sandwich wrapped in plastic in front of each of us. As they drove away, in a brief flash I crossed time and space: I saw through the metal and plastic of the car, I saw through her flesh. The creature slept in there, new skull soft and bulging. I began to cry. Seeing me cry, you started, too. Together, there under the willow tree, among empty soda bottles and dog waste, we wore out our lungs. Nothing is worse than the vision of your own obsolescence.

Bez alkoholu
DOM SZCZĘŚLIWY

My Crush on Hilary Duff

BLAZE GINSBERG

In 2002, Blaze Ginsberg was the subject of Raising Blaze, *his mother's account of her efforts to shepherd him through the public-school system. The book covered eight years, from kindergarten through seventh grade, during which Blaze was judged at various times to have learning disabilities, behavioral problems, autism, ADHD, Asperger's syndrome, and an assortment of other conditions, without ever being definitively diagnosed. (Last year, Blaze did receive a formal diagnosis, of high-functioning autism.)*

In 2005, Blaze began writing his own book. Arranged in the style of internet episode guides, his autobiography describes his life as a series of TV shows in which he's appeared. The full book, entitled Episodes, *will be published in the fall of 2009 by Roaring Brook Press; what follows is one chapter, a romance, which ran from 2004 to 2006.*

SEASON 1

Episode 1: Pilot
Air Date: 5-1-2004
I wake up in the morning and watch *Lizzie McGuire* on ABC Kids and decide I'm going to be a fan of Hilary Duff. The game I'm playing that month is *Monsters, Inc.*, and I'm dedicating it to Hilary Duff. This is like Mom when she was writing her book in 1993 and listening to Madonna a lot for inspiration. Well, it returns eleven years later with my playing *Monsters, Inc.* constantly. I go for a swim at Nana and Papa's pool. I'm however thinking about Hilary a lot.

Episode 2: The Next Day
Air Date: 5-2-2004
I go out with Déja to the mall and bring up Hilary Duff. We go for a drive to the La Jolla AMC parking garage and later on when I'm having a problem I pretend there is a paper on my sleeve that says "I love Hilary Duff."
Notes: Throughout that month I watch *Lizzie McGuire* and support my fanhood of Hilary. On Nana's birthday, May 15, 2004, I see *Metamorphosis*, her first album, for

the first time. I am telling people at school that I'm a fan and I get some reactions. Crystal tells me Lizzie McGuire is her cousin. Preston calls and pretends to be Hilary on the phone and convinces me it's her. David M. tells me he watches the show too. They are teasing me into a riot.

Quotes: Me: "If Hilary Duff hated *The Nutcracker* I'd pay her eighteen dollars."

Déja: "You'd pay her eighteen dollars?"

Episode 3: First Big Movie
Air Date: 7-16-2004

I go to see *A Cinderella Story* with Maya. I enjoy Hilary's performance. It's my first movie as a fan of hers.

Episode 4: Now There's a Hottie You Don't See Every Day
Air Date: 7-23-2004

It's my birthday; number seventeen. My first present is a Dana (a kind of laptop) from Mom. After that there is some slight commotion, and then I leave for my massage at Debby's house. We get there and my massage is relaxing for half an hour. When that's over Maya drops me off with Déja, who takes me to Target. I am very reluctant to go to Target on my birthday. But we go. I get a chess set, *Dude, Where's My Car?*, and Monopoly. Then Déja takes me home. Gabe is supposed to come over, and I'm very anxious for him to arrive because I am expecting *Metamorphosis* as a present from him. He finally does. I open one of his two gifts; it's *The Sandlot*. Then the second gift, the grand prize: *Metamorphosis*. We get

ready to go to the beach, but before we leave my uncle Bo arrives. With a poster of *her*. This day is where my fanhood of Hilary Duff is really getting serious. Then we leave for the beach and I put *Metamorphosis* on in the car. We hang at the beach then we go home to Lavander, who is on the couch. Her gifts are *The Cheetah Girls* and *The Matrix Reloaded*.

Notes: There was a cake with white frosting; my favorite.

Quotes: Papa: "I need to talk to him now that he's seventeen."

Episode 5: Oh Hilary
Air Date: 7-24-2004

The next day: who what when why where how my mind was set from sunrise to sunset from the minute I got up to the minute I went down. Hilary Duff, that's right. I didn't obsess about anything else: not the mysterious Motown song I've been desperately trying to find for years; not the sandwich deal that had been going the past three years (Mom will not let me go on a hot-air-balloon ride until I eat a sandwich); not even how Crystal stabbed me in the back on the second day of school. None of that mattered on July 24, 2004, because Hilary Duff had me. Back then, if I could have I'd have given my life to her. I go home, watch *Dude, Where's My Car?*, and then Déja picks me up for Dillon and Asher's birthday celebrations. Then I go with my friend Michael to see a musical called *Route 66*. After that I go home for the night.

Episode 6: What a Dream
Air Date: 7-28-2004

I have a dream that Hilary Duff is in my school. Later in the dream I am cuddling with her.

Episode 7: There You Are, Girl
Air Date: 8-14-2004

Mom comes home with a calendar of Hilary Duff for me. Fifteen months of Hilary. I go lie down on my bed while I wait for Bo to pick me up and go out. I cuddle with a pillow and pretend it's her.
Notes: From today until the end of 2005, Hilary is going to be on my wall.
Quotes: Mom: "Hilary Duff!!!!!!!!!!!!!!!!!!!!!!"

Episode 8: Hilary Is Worth Something
Air Date: 11-28-2004

I am out with Bo and he stops at Circuit City and is in there for a long while. I wait in his truck. When he comes out, he's bought me a *The Girl Can Rock* CD. Hilary again.
Quotes: Bo: "I'm the best uncle."

Episode 9: In My Mind
Air Date: 12-11-2004

I go on my first visit to Déja's apartment in Pasadena where she had moved with her boyfriend (now ex), Kevin. I talk about Hilary Duff. I play my first-ever game of *Grand Theft Auto*. In bed that night, I listen to a couple of tracks of her album.

Quotes: Me: "I imagine Hilary Duff singing the fourth track on her album at sunset."

Episode 10: The Trouble with Hilary's Singing Style
Air Date: 12-12-2004

I am having a slight problem with Hilary's singing style and get worried I will end up like Tia on that one episode of *Sister, Sister* where she and her boyfriend broke up. But I manage to bear with it.

Quotes: Me: "I am having a slight problem with Hilary Duff's singing style. She sings one part of the song over and over again."

Mom: "Is it like that Bill Withers song, 'I know, I know, I know, I know'?"
Me: "No."

Episode 11: Hilary Times Hilary
Air Date: 12-25-2004

Christmas. It's my first Christmas with me being crushed over Hilary Duff. I receive two gifts related to her. One is a photo collage that Kevin made for me. When I see one of the pictures has what looks like a guy in it, I presume it's her boyfriend in real life. False alarm. For a minute my crush on Hilary Duff was just inches away from getting axed—I felt like ripping those pictures to bits. But it survived that brush with death. My second gift is *A Cinderella Story* on DVD.

Episode 12: Go Haylie
Air Date: 2-25-2005

A fluke occurs: Haylie Duff is crying on *Joan of Arcadia* as Stevie Marx. This is very unusual. In the past nine months I have only been crushed over Hilary. Now I have to think about her sister.

Episode 13: Off My Girl
Air Date: 3-9-2005

I am out with Lavander at Red Robin and we are having a nice time until she says this: "Guess what? Hilary Duff has a boyfriend." She continues, "Guess how old he is? Twenty-seven." I am not happy to hear this news but she even agrees with me that they need to break up. I go for my second visit to Déja's apartment in Pasadena.

Quotes: Kevin: "I know about her boyfriend."

SEASON 2

Episode 14: A Year Ago Today
Air Date: 5-1-2005

It's been one year since the start of my crush. I talk about it a lot. Instead of going on a Saturday Groove this weekend (the Saturday Groove is when we pick up Nana on Saturday morning and go for tea, shopping, and driving), we go on a Sunday Groove this time, to the mall. After that, we stop at Chevy's and eat.

Notes: This is the night that I was worried David M. was going to kill me because he threatened me on the bus.

Episode 15: The First Group Meeting
Air Date: 9-4-2005

Group is a time for us to get together with a counselor and talk about life and how it is affecting us. I have been dying to know who the new group members are going to be. Last year it was me, Josh, Mike, and Bill. This year it's me, Seth, and Bill. We talk about our lives. Unfortunately Seth's mother died in 2002. But group goes wonderfully.

Notes: First mention of Hilary Duff in group.

Quotes: Me: "Have any of you ever heard of *Lizzie McGuire*? As some of you know, I have a crush on Hilary Duff."

Seth: "My mother died from multiple sclerosis."

Episode 16: Severe Crush Damage
Air Date: 9-9-2005

I'm out walking with mom and we run into an *OK!* magazine with an article about Hilary Duff and her home life. I don't want to get it but Mom buys it for me. I read about Hilary and her boyfriend Joel Madden and I am disgusted. This time I let it ruin my day. I obsess about it like Michael with his OCD. Threats for my crush to be axed are bad today, worse than ever before.

Notes: Two years ago, my friend Brittany left the school and today I feel the same way I did then.

Quotes: Mom: "I want you to focus more on Kelly Clarkson."

Me: "She's five years older than me."

Mom: "So? I'm sick of hearing about Hilary Duff."

Episode 17: Teen Music Fever
Air Date: 10-21-2005

In PE one day I talk with Coach about my Hilary Duff thing. I ask him how old he is. We sing "Since U Been Gone" by Kelly Clarkson and we discuss what we will sing at the talent show. Later that night I buy a remixed version of Kelly Clarkson's song on iTunes. The whole album was different remixes of that one song.

Notes: Coach is twelve years older than I am. He was born in May 1975. Jason Nevins was the main remix person of Kelly Clarkson's 2004 hit "Since U Been Gone."

Trivia: I end up performing "I Won't Back Down" by Tom Petty at the talent show, which was in May. That goes well.

Episode 18: Hilary's Latest and Greatest
Air Date: 12-30-2005

I am in Ralph's Coffee Shop. I'm feeling bad for my friend Sarah in Lower School because her dog got eaten by a coyote, but then I see a magazine article about the true-life story of Hilary Duff and read a little about Joel Madden. This time I am able to read it without getting disgusted. I even learn about Joel Madden. He has a twin brother, an older brother, and a younger sister. Later on, Déja buys Hilary Duff's album *Most Wanted* for me.

Episode 19: The Same Old
Air Date: 12-31-2005
It's about to be the New Year and Hilary Duff is hosting *New Year's Eve Live*. Her voice sounds really different. She sings "Beat of My Heart." I lie in bed and watch her. Unfortunately, Green Day interrupts the session with Hilary and I'm really irritated.
Quotes: Mom: "She just keeps singing the same thing over and over—'beat of my heart, beat of my heart, beat of my heart.'"

Episode 20: Let's Get This Movie on the Road
Air Date: 3-5-2006
Bo buys me *The Perfect Man* on DVD. My collection is now as follows: *The Lizzie McGuire Movie*, the poster, the collage, *Cheaper by the Dozen*, *A Cinderella Story*, *Raise Your Voice*, and last but not least, *The Perfect Man*. I don't really know how I feel about *The Perfect Man*.

Episode 21: I Live It Again
Air Date: 4-1-2006
It's been twenty-three months since I became a fan of Hilary Duff. It's a Saturday. I go for a driving lesson with Gabe and then go out to the 99-cent store in Encinitas with Mom and Nana. Then I go out with Bo. We go to the hot tub, the sauna, and the pool. He calls this "The Jewish Triathlon."
Notes: Andrea Barber plays Kimmy Gibbler on *Full House*. I've been watching this show in syndication for a while. On this day I become a fan of hers, but only for one day.

Episode 22: That Movie Rocks (Wrapping the Crush)
Air Date: 8-18-2006 (Part 1)
The day that *Material Girls* opens I go to see it with Maya. In that movie Hilary and Haylie Duff play two sisters who go broke. Today it seems like everything related to Hilary has happened before:
    1. Hilary and Haylie being in the same movie together
    2. Haylie Duff crying
    3. Hilary crying constantly like in *Raise Your Voice*

4. Haylie having a spell on me

5. Hilary Duff singing

6. Another star of *Lizzie McGuire* starring in the movie with Hil

Except for two new things:

1. Hilary performing a song by another artist—"Material Girl" by Madonna

2. Hilary going to jail in the movie

This is like the last episode of *Full House*, which was titled "Michelle Rides Again." In this series finale, Joey, Uncle Jesse, and Danny try to reboot Michelle's memory after she falls off her horse. All the regulars who had ever starred on the show appeared in the last few minutes of the series. Today, almost all crush events appear on the last episode of my crush on Hilary Duff. It ends the same way *Full House* did but eleven years later.

Episode 23: That Movie Rocks (Wrapping the Crush)
Air Date: 8-18-2006 (Part 2)

I enjoy the movie as today is the last day of my crush on Hilary Duff. It was as if the spirits knew that today was going to be the day where my crush ended. I've been listening to Jimi Hendrix singing "Red House." The last lyric says, "If my baby don't love me no more, I know her sister will." I consider doing this with Haylie and potentially being crushed over Haylie, maybe in a couple of years. Later on the movie ends and right there is where my crush on Hilary Duff ends for good. I decided to end it because she didn't have much work this year and I have been interested in other girls. Josh had a very hard time believing this when I told him.

Back when I first became cyber-buddies with Sarah C., I kind of knew that this was going to be the last event of my crush on Hilary Duff. But then it was uncertain for a while what was going to happen. But then, official decision: Today it ends.

Notes: This episode was split into two parts because I had to go to the bathroom in the middle of *Material Girls*.

Quotes: Maya: "I think Haylie's a better actress than Hilary."

Me (*last line of the series*): "Jimi Hendrix is in the house."

Special: My Life On
Air Date: 8-26-2006

I start college and meet a girl, Alexis, in yoga. That goes well. I have developed a friendly relationship and plan to start off as just friends. And we are off to a good start so far. Down at Jimbo's Market, a goth girl named Tiana has been checking me out a lot and scanning my items. Josh comes into town to visit and we have words about how my crush on Hilary Duff ended. At college I also meet Sarah A. who I help get a soda when it is stuck in the machine. She's a potential girlfriend for about thirty seconds. At work I meet a girl, Anna, who claims to be my number-one fan. I ask her out on a date but she says she is focusing on school and is not dating. But I did ask her.

My crush on Hilary Duff was a legend. From 2004 to 2006 it was the line of entertainment for the Ginsberg family. It exists now only in memory after dying of natural causes.

~ In memory of my crush on Hilary Duff ~
2004–2006
Series status: Cancelled

The Painting

RODDY DOYLE

CHAPTER ONE

Adam came to Ireland because it was a rich country but also because it was an island. It would never change. True, the sea would batter its coast and take some land and make new land somewhere else. Also true, global warming would bring with it unpleasant consequences, and the sea would soon enough creep up the streets and little roads. But, nevertheless, what attracted Adam to Ireland was its dependability. Dublin, where he now lived, would always be on the east coast. Athlone, where he had not yet been, would always be in the center. Adam valued permanence.

He did not regret leaving Poland. He had grown up in the town of Bialystok, in the east. In the time of his grandfather, it had been nearer the west. In the generation before that, there had been no Poland. And again, for some time in his father's childhood, Poland had ceased to exist. Adam himself remembered clearly the excitement and noise among the adults as the Berlin Wall came down and Poland became, again, a different place. Poland never stayed still. But Ireland did. That was why he was in Dublin, Ireland's capital, in the late autumn. And that was why he had bought a yard brush.

The leaves had started to fall. Adam stood at his only window and watched them slide and gather and disperse, along both sides of the street and down its center, under the Jeeps and Volvos, and carried in the wind, over garden walls and past his window. They never stayed still.

Adam was an artist. His work was often called "precise." The precision impressed, and quite often frightened, people who looked or even glanced at the paintings.

—How did he do that?

—It's more exact than a photograph.

—There's something evil about it; let's get out of here.

The street disappeared under the thick carpet of leaves. Yet no one seemed to care. Women parked their sports cars on top of hills made of leaves. Old ladies stood still, surrounded by leaves, and waited for the wind to blow a pathway for them. Men came home carrying laptop bags and brown paper bags full of wine and cheese. But Adam saw no one carry a broom.

Adam painted only what was permanent. It was why he painted. Stones. Cliffs. Cathedrals, bridges. He had painted ruins, but only after they had stayed unalterably ruined for hundreds of years. He accepted slow change; he realized that time would not stand still. But sudden things—fireworks, puberty, death, the snow that blanketed Poland, suddenly, in a matter of hours every year—they all upset him. He had lost his father, suddenly, his mother, suddenly, his brother, grandmother, girlfriends, several jobs, his house keys, many times—all suddenly.

The Irish leaves fell like Polish snow. But, unlike snow, shockingly unlike snow, they lifted, fell, dispersed, regathered, became the rustlings of Adam's nightmares. They never settled and let him rest. He lay down but he could not sleep. The drug addict in the room next to Adam's played the greatest hits of Tina Turner until two hours after dawn. But it was not the adult-oriented rock that kept Adam awake. He liked Tina Turner. All those years, she had never changed. No; it was the leaves.

Adam bought the broom. He could not afford it. But, as he stood on the windy street, he was almost happy. He started outside the house of an old woman. He swept the leaves off the path.

—Hey.

He turned and saw, not the old woman, but a much younger, very attractive woman.

—Are you from the Council? she asked.

—No, said Adam.

—Then piss off, said the woman. —Go on.

Her hostility was a shock. Adam had hoped that his sweeping would be welcomed. His new neighbors would smile and wave and he, in turn, would smile and wave. He was a lonely man, and shy. By providing this help, he would become a neighbor.

But Adam's help wasn't wanted.

—Why are you doing that?

—You're only making it worse.

He gave up.

He stood at his window and watched as a man from

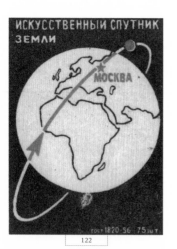

the City Council came down the street and swept away most of the leaves. No one came out and objected. Adam had never felt more isolated and alone.

But then he got a job.

It was quite an unusual job. He had to pretend that he was a student of art.

—But I am already an artist, said Adam.

—My friend, said his new employer, —that does not matter. Listen. You ring the bell and when it is answered, you say these words to the nice lady who stands there: "I am a student from Russia, do you want to see my paintings?"

CHAPTER TWO

Every morning, Adam stood under the iron railway bridge beside the river. He waited for his employer's minibus. He stood with four other young men. A Latvian, two Lithuanians, and an extremely tall man from the Czech Republic. Like Adam, they had to pretend that they were Russian art students.

Their employer, who actually was Russian, explained it to them.

—My friends, he said, —you come here from countries which are in E.U. You call at doors with paintings, the ladies say "Get real jobs, there are many jobs." But if you are Russian, you come from somewhere wild. You have escape. You have sympathy.

Their employer's smiling eyes filled the rearview mirror.

—I choose you because you are thin men, he told them.

It was true. The young men in the minibus were thin.

—You are thin, handsome men.

This also was true. The thin young men in the mini-bus were handsome.

—The Irish ladies will wish to make you fat.

But this was not true. The Irish ladies had no wish to feed or fatten Adam. The ladies and gentlemen did not wish to buy, or even see, his paintings.

—No.

—You're jestin'.

—No, thanks.

All day, for many days, Adam rang bells and knocked on doors. His hand felt heavy as he lifted it. He was very

shy. But he was also hungry. So, every time a door opened, he smiled or tried to smile and said,

—I am a student from Russia, do you want to see my paintings?

—No.

—Not today.

—I already have paintings.

Adam carried his portfolio, stuffed with other people's art, across squares, along avenues, down Dublin's many cul-de-sacs. The Eskimos, it is said, have two hundred words for snow. The Irish had many words for no.

—My ma's not here.

—I left my glasses at work.

—Ah, lovely.

—You're grand.

—Bye-bye.

Only three times in six days did ladies wish to see the paintings. Adam unzipped the portfolio, trying not to look at the art. He flicked from picture to picture.

—You like?

—They're a bit bright, said a lady in Foxrock.

—They're a bit passé, said a lady in Blackrock.

—They're a bit shite, said a lady in Coolock.

And, sadly, Adam agreed.

Every evening, their employer would drive the young men back to the iron bridge beside the river. His mirrored eyes would go to each young man.

—You had much success today, my friend?

Adam always sat in the seat right behind his employer. The other young men had quickly learned that this was Adam's place. He no longer had to push or race to get there first.

—Two paintings, said the very tall Czech.

—Very good.

—Three paintings, said the Latvian.

—Good.

—Four, said one of the Lithuanians.

—Also four, said his compatriot.

—Good, good, said their employer.

His eyes were now on Adam. So were the eyes of the other young men.

—No paintings, said Adam.

—Alas, my friend, said his employer. —No food, no beer, no fun.

He smiled. But it wasn't a nasty smile; he was not a nasty man.

—Tomorrow, he said, —you will have good luck.

—Perhaps, said Adam, —I can show some of my paintings?

—My friend, said his employer. —No.

—But, said Adam.

He slapped the portfolio on his lap.

—These paintings are not good.

This was true. The art was derivative and sentimental, but also quite disturbing—Hallmark cards, by Salvador Dalí. Melting rabbits. Lovers under a melting sun. Many things melted in these paintings. Adam could not look at them.

—My friend, said Adam's employer. —I do not agree.

The mirrored eyes were fixed on Adam.

—You would like to know why?

Adam nodded. —Yes.

—*I* painted these paintings, said his employer.

He laughed, and the other young men eventually laughed.

—I am sorry, said Adam.

—For sure, said his employer. —It is not problem for me. For *you*, I guess, it is problem.

They had reached the bridge and the river. He stopped the minibus. He turned in his seat and looked at Adam.

—One more day, he said. —We see if you can sell some Russian paintings. You understand, my friend?

—Yes, said Adam.

—You want to do this?

—Yes, said Adam.

So, the following morning, Adam waited at the railway bridge, with the other young men. They nodded, but they did not speak to him. The minibus arrived. The young men climbed in, and their employer drove to a part

of the city that, to Adam, became increasingly familiar. He was going back the way he had come, to the tree-lined street where he now lived. As he stepped out of the minibus, a large, brown, very dry leaf, one of the last leaves on the street, was lifted by the wind and slapped Adam crisply across the face.

CHAPTER THREE

Adam started at No. 1. He insisted on it.

—But why not this house, said his employer, pointing at the large, red-bricked house nearest them. —There are many walls for paintings.

But Adam pointed up the long straight street, to a point somewhere beyond the line of leafless trees.

—This is better for me, he said.

His employer shrugged, and held the portfolio out to Adam.

—My friend, he said. —This is the day you make or you break. You understand this?

—Yes, said Adam.

He patted Adam's shoulder.

—Tonight we will be very rich men, I think.

He watched Adam walk away, up the hill. He wondered if he would ever see Adam again. Something about the way Adam walked—he looked like a man who was going all the way to Poland.

But he didn't. He walked—he *trudged*—until he came to the first house on the

street, No. 1. He saw no bell, so he knocked on the door. No one answered. He crossed the street, to No. 2. No one answered. Adam crossed and recrossed the street many times, until he came to No. 37. It was the house of one of the old ladies. He opened the gate and heard its rusty shriek. He knew this noise. He had heard it often as he lay in bed. Now that he knew its source, he would buy some oil and, secretly, late at night, lubricate the gate's painful hinges.

He walked to the door. He rang the bell. He heard it faintly from deep inside the house. He heard heels cross the wooden floor. He saw a human shape, the old lady, behind the door's frosted glass. He stood back. The door opened.

But it wasn't an old lady. It was the young woman who had been rude to Adam weeks before, when the leaves were falling.

She was still very attractive. Also, Adam quickly noticed and approved: she was wearing the very same clothes she had worn when she'd told him to piss off that day. This time, however, her words were different.

—Hi there, she said.

—I am a student from Russia, said Adam. —Do you want to see my paintings?

—Cool, she said.

—You do?

—Yeah, she said. —Go on.

She seemed eager. She stared at the portfolio. Adam wondered if she was mocking him. He fumbled with the zip. He placed the bottom of the portfolio at his feet, on his shoes, and let the front cover drop. He watched her look at the first dreadful painting and its many melting cats and dogs.

—Cool, she said.

—You like it? said Adam.

She shrugged. He liked the way her shoulders moved under her carefully torn black jumper.

—You wish to buy it? said Adam.

—No way, she said. —Show us the next one.

Adam let the first painting in its plastic cover drop. She gazed at the next one.

—Wow, she said.

She looked at him.

—And you did this, yeah? she asked.

—Yes, Adam lied.

—It's amazing, she said.

Adam looked down at the melting sun dripping upon the lovers on the purple riverbank. He felt ashamed, and very pleased. He saw the admiration on her face. It was a beautiful face; a reliable face. The adjustments in expression were minimal but clear.

—You wish to buy? said Adam.

—No, she said.

She walked away from the open door.

—Come in, she said as she went.

Adam bent down and closed the portfolio. When he looked up the young woman had gone. The long hall was empty.

He stepped in. He listened. He thought he heard something, a clattering of some kind, deeper into the house. He closed the door. It was quite dark in the hall, and silent. He walked. He heard his steps. He could hear no other sound. He passed two closed doors, and a third, and a fourth. He felt something brush his face. A loose cobweb, he thought. He came to some stone steps, down, and another door. This door was partially open. He pushed.

—What kept you?

She sat beside a fire.

—Show me more, she said. —Come on.

Adam stood in front of the girl and the fire. Again, he unzipped the black portfolio. Again, he let it rest on his shoes. Again, he let the plastic-covered paintings drop. The cats and dogs, the sun and the lovers, the melting cars.

—Cool.

The melting rabbits.

—Cruel.

She sat up. She leaned closer to the falling paintings. It was as if Adam was pulling her toward him. The melting fruit, the melting woman.

—Wait, wait!

—You wish to buy this one? said Adam.

She held the painting. She brought it closer to her beautiful, unchanging face. She threw it into the fire.

CHAPTER FOUR

It happened very quickly. Before Adam could decide to save the painting, it was much too late. He watched the flames climb across the melting woman and consume her.

—You burned the painting, he said.

—It was melting anyway, said the young woman.

—But, said Adam. —It costs €50.

—Great value, said the young woman.

—You will pay?

—No way, she said. —Paint me.

Her face was calm, quite imperturbable. Adam was not certain that he had actually heard her speak.

—You wish for me to paint you? he asked.

—Yeah, she said.

She sat quite still, looking straight at Adam.

—You wish to melt in this painting? he asked.

—Don't think so, she said.

Adam did not like painting portraits. Faces sneezed, grew beards and fat. Faces aged and fell apart. Even in sleep, faces shifted and jumped. No one ever stayed still. But this woman seemed to.

—You will pay? said Adam.

—If you paint me?

—Yes.

—Ah yeah, she said.

Adam did not ask how much. He did not want to change his mind.

—Yes, said Adam. —I agree to do this.

—Cool, said the woman.

—Yes.

—What's your name? said the woman.

—Adam.

—No way.

—Yes, said Adam. —I am Adam.

—Jesus, said the woman. —That's amazing. My name's Eve.

—That is a very good one, said Adam.

—Yeah, said the woman called Eve. —Will you start tomorrow then?

—Yes, said Adam. —Tomorrow.

—Cool, said the woman. —Bye.

She did not move. She did not speak again.

Adam stood up.

—Goodbye, he said.

Eve did not respond.

He closed her front door, very quietly. He walked to the gate. Again, he heard its rusty shriek. He walked home. He sold no more paintings that day. He did not try to sell any. He lay on his bed. He thought about this woman, Eve. He thought about her face, and paint.

As the time approached to meet his employer, Adam finally got off the bed. He lifted the mattress and took his last €50 note from under it. He put on his jacket— it was raining hard outside.

His employer sat in the minibus and blew cigarette smoke into the rain.

—My friend, said his employer. —You sold some paintings today?

—I sold one painting, said Adam.

—Which painting?

—Naked woman, melting.

—Very good, said his employer. —My wife. She will be very happy. Good times for me, I think.

He laughed. And Adam heard the other men behind him laugh, deep inside the minibus.

Adam handed him the €50 note through the open window. He opened the sliding door of the minibus and placed the portfolio inside, against the seat back. He shut the door. He stood in the rain.

—Goodbye, he said.

He waved to the young men looking out at him.

—You don't get in? said his employer.

—No, said Adam.

His ex-employer shrugged, and smiled, and blew smoke past Adam's shoulder.

—Maybe it is best, he said.

He started the minibus.

—I wish you luck.

—Thank you, said Adam.

He watched until the minibus turned left, onto the main road, then walked back to his room. He turned on his radio and ate two cans of spaghetti hoops. He heard none of the radio news stories. All the time, he was thinking of the woman, Eve. He had no more money, he had no more food—he was hungry again—and, yet, all he could think of was the woman, sitting still, sitting very, very still.

It was dark when Adam stood up. It had been dark for many hours—it was after midnight. He put on his jacket and left his room. He brought with him a bottle of olive oil.

He walked to No. 37, the house where Eve lived. He stopped outside. He was alone on the street. All the windows he saw were dark or curtained. He gently pushed the gate. It shrieked, as it had done earlier that day. Adam poured the olive oil onto its hinges. He pulled the gate, and pushed. It no longer shrieked. He crossed the street, to another gate that he had heard shriek. He oiled this gate too, and other gates, until the bottle was empty.

He was hungry when he finally fell asleep, and he was hungry when he woke. He was hungry, and nervous, as he walked to No. 37. The front gate opened silently.

He was hungry as he rang the bell. Once again, he heard it faintly from deep inside the house. He heard heels cross the wooden floor. He saw the shape, Eve, behind the door's frosted glass. The door opened. The aroma—bacon, sausages—surrounded him, assaulted him.

—Oh, hi there, she said. —Come in.

CHAPTER FIVE

Adam shut the front door, and when he turned she'd gone again, as if she'd never been there. A beautiful, ghostlike woman, who left in her wake the very real aroma of bacon and sausage. The full Irish breakfast. Adam was in love.

He followed the smell and the woman down the dark hall, to the kitchen.

He pushed open the door.

She sat at the table, looking down. The morning sun filled the big window behind her, and lit her hair. And the steam rising from the plate in front of her—she looked as if she was on fire. She was, Adam decided—and he knew

this to be true—the most beautiful woman he had ever seen.

But she ate like a pig and she offered him nothing.

He stood at the door and watched her eat. Three sausages, two fried eggs, five of the thin slices of bacon that in Ireland were called rashers. And toast. Lots of toast, many slices, one by one. Adam watched the butter drip onto the table. He watched her wipe the white plate with the second-to-last slice of toast. He watched her eat it. And he watched her eat the last slice, after she'd wiped the table with it. The plate and table were clean. The smell, however, still tortured him.

—That's better, she said. —I was starving.

She was looking at him.

—Where's the thing? she asked.

—Thing? said Adam. —What thing, please?

—The thing, she said. —For putting the painting on. You're supposed to, like, look at me from behind it, yeah?

—Do you mean the easel? said Adam.

—Yeah, she said. —Where is it?

—In Poland, said Adam.

She looked disappointed, almost angry.

—I am sorry, said Adam.

—Bummer, said Eve. —Do you even have any paints and stuff?

—I have a pencil, said Adam.

—No way, said Eve. —Is that all?

Adam took the pencil from his back pocket.

—It is a very good pencil, he said.

He held up his drawing pad.

—I wish to do some sketches first, he said.

This was true. Also true was the fact that Adam had no paints, and no money to buy any.

She still hadn't moved.

But now she did. She was out of her chair before he'd noticed her moving. The white plate was in her hand. Then she threw it. Adam saw it fly across the kitchen. It landed in the sink, *smack*, on top of the water. He watched sudsy water rise, then drop. The suds stayed in the air and caught the light. The sudden violence, the happy ending—Adam thought he'd die. His heart fell into his very empty stomach.

—So, she said. —Okay.

She turned to Adam.

—So, sketch then. Where do you want me?

Adam took one step into the kitchen. Eve held no more plates or missiles.

—Well? she said. —Am I okay here?

—No, said Adam.

She was too flimsy, too ghostlike, against the white sunlight that filled the window. She'd shimmer and drift, like steam—like the suds—before he'd even started.

He walked to the window. He saw the cord, and pulled down the canvas blind.

—But the sun, she protested.

—Not good, said Adam.

The sun was now a gray block, behind the canvas. It looked solid, already painted. Adam picked up a chair and moved it to the left of the block of canvas light.

—Sit here, please, he said.

—I want to stand, said Eve —It's more me.

—You will stand for many hours, perhaps. And you must not move.

—Oh, okay, she said. —Will I stick on some music first?

—No, said Adam.

—Why not?

He didn't want to tell her that he couldn't listen to music that he hadn't already heard many times before. And he guessed that she was not a great admirer of the songs of Tina Turner. So—

—My tone is deaf, he said.

—What does that mean? she said, as she sat. —You can't make out the notes?

—Yes, said Adam.

She sang.

—I'M YOUR PRIVATE DANCER—DANCER FOR MONEY—What did that sound like?

Wonderful, he thought.

—I did not hear it, he said. —You sang?

—Yeah, she said. —Jesus; you poor thing.

133

Adam shrugged.

—It does not matter so much, he said.

—Were you always like that? she asked.

And Adam made a decision. He gave her the interesting answer.

—No, he said.

He moved a chair, and sat. He felt suddenly powerful. He almost laughed.

—What happened? Eve asked.

He did not know yet how he would respond. He stared at the white page, then at her. He looked down at the page again. His stomach growled.

—Is it difficult to talk about? she asked.

He nodded, and then started to draw.

CHAPTER SIX

Eve stayed silent, and still. And Adam drew. But he did not draw Eve. He couldn't. He couldn't look at her properly yet. He could not gaze.

He drew Bugs Bunny and a carrot.

—How's it going? she asked, after four long minutes.

—Quite well, said Adam.

—Can I see?

She stood up.

—No! said Adam—he shouted.

He turned his page quickly. She heard it rip.

—I must start again, said Adam.

—Sorry, said Eve.

She sat.

Adam drew another rabbit. He looked at Eve, and down. He drew a window beside the rabbit's head. He started on the carrot.

—Sorry, she said, again.

He knew; she wanted him to speak. It was a fresh carrot, straight from the ground. Leaves sprang from it, longer than the carrot itself.

—It is okay, said Adam.

He looked at Eve. His stomach growled. He looked down again.

—Are you hungry? Eve asked.

—No, said Adam.

The smell of bacon still floated throughout the room. Adam drew a pig beside the rabbit. He looked at Eve. He drew a dark line quickly through the pig. He turned the page.

—Am I hard? Eve asked.

—Hard?

—To draw, said Eve.

—No, said Adam.

—Am I talking too much?

No, he thought.

—Yes, he said.

He loved her voice but he couldn't look at her while she spoke. She was too lively, too alive.

The page was empty. He resisted; he didn't draw a rabbit, or anything else. He looked at Eve. She stayed still. He drew a line. He drew another line. He drew a chin. It was nothing like her chin, or any chin. His stomach howled. He drew four quick lines—the window. He looked again, at her boots. They were black, but unpolished. They looked solid and ancient. The laces were undone.

—What're you looking at? she said.

It was a question he had often heard in this city, and he'd learned quite quickly that it wasn't really a question. *What are you bleedin' lookin' at?* He had tried to answer it the first time he'd been asked, by a young man who was climbing out of a sports car.

—I look at your car, Adam had said.

—Why? said the young man. —D'you think I robbed it or somethin'?

—No, Adam had said.

Since then, he'd avoided the question by never looking too carefully at anyone or anything, or stopping to look.

This time, though, the question was different. It was a real question; Eve was curious.

—I look at your boots, Adam told her.

He could draw the boots. They'd been there for a thousand years; that was how they looked. He could start with the boots. They were like solid, permanent rock.

—What about them? she asked.

Adam shrugged.

—They are on your feet, he said. —So I must draw them. Please do not move.

So Adam drew a pair of boots. He drew the boots, but he looked at the woman wearing the boots. He drew; he looked. She looked, she waited—she didn't move. It was more than an hour before she spoke again.

—I have to go to work, she said. —Can I look?

—No, said Adam.

—Ah—

—Not yet, said Adam.

She stood up.

—Please, said Adam. —Please. Do not throw a plate.

—I wasn't going to, she said.

—Thank you, said Adam.

She muttered something about being hungry. Adam watched her go to the big refrigerator. She opened it and, for some seconds, Adam thought she had climbed in. She had disappeared.

He waited. She will invite me to share her lunch, he thought—he hoped. He prayed.

—Goodbye, he said.

—Yeah, bye, she said.

Her voice boomed beautifully from deep within the fridge. Adam waited some more seconds, then left. He was starving, literally, but he was also very happy. He was ecstatic. Boots floated all around him. Where once there had been leaves, there were boots—black boots in the wind, falling slowly to the ground.

—Are you all right there?

It was an old woman. She was looking at Adam. Her face was very close to his. She was leaning over, he slowly realized. He was lying on the ground. He looked left and right—no boots. He'd fainted—he must have fainted.

—Are you all right? the old woman asked again.

—I am quite well, said Adam.

—You're hungry, aren't you?

—Yes, said Adam. —I am very hungry.

—See now, she said. —I knew.

She stood back.

—Come on, she said.

She stood back, but her face remained close to Adam's. He sat up. He saw now that the old woman was bent over, as if carrying a great weight across the center of her back.

He stood up. He followed her—back to the house he'd just come from.

CHAPTER SEVEN

Through the same front door, down the dark, narrow hall, Adam followed the old woman to the kitchen.

The empty kitchen.

Adam was surprised. Perhaps he had been asleep on the path, deep in the dream of the falling boots, for a quite a long time. But he did not think so. He had fainted, but only for some seconds. The light at the window confirmed it; very little time had passed since he'd last looked at it.

But where was Eve?

The smell of bacon was still fresh and cruel.

Where was Eve?

—Stay there, said the old woman, —till we see what's in this thing.

She stood at the fridge, her old head below the handle, and opened it.

—Not much, she said. —She nearly ate the lot.

She reappeared from behind the door, carrying a box of eggs.

—Two left.

She went behind the counter, and Adam saw the frying pan lifted onto the hob. He saw the hand holding the pan,

but not the woman. He saw the old hand tap one egg, then the other, against the side of the pan. He watched the eggs drop onto the pan.

The old woman came out from behind the counter.

—I used to be as tall as her, she said. —Would you believe that?

—Yes, said Adam.

—And better looking, she said. —What do you think of that?

—I believe it is the truth, said Adam.

—I'm sure you do, said the old woman.

She turned back to the eggs. She disappeared behind the counter.

—You are her grandmother? Adam asked.

—I am.

She waddled from behind the counter, carrying a plate exactly like the one Eve had thrown. She brought the plate to the table. Adam followed her.

—Here now, she said.

—Thank you, said Adam.

Adam had never liked eggs; they were too runny and difficult to control. But he quickly changed his mind. These eggs were not runny. He sliced them, and they stayed sliced. He ate them quickly, and they stayed eaten. He was still hungry, but he was no longer starving to death.

He turned, and saw the old woman looking at his sketches, the unsuccessful faces and the boots.

—You'll need money for your paints, she said. —Won't you?

—Yes, said Adam.

—Here.

He saw now, there was a €50 note in one of her hands. She shook the note.

—Take it, she said.

She sounded, he thought just then, very like Eve's grandmother.

He took the money.

—Thank you.

—Do a good job, mind, said the old woman.

—Yes.

—The boots were mine, you know, she said.

—Yes?

The old woman sighed.

—She hasn't spoken to me in years.

—I beg your pardon, said Adam. —What is your name?

—I don't matter, said the old woman. —Just do a good job.

—I will, said Adam.

—You're a handsome man, she said. —But skinny.

—I must go now, said Adam.

—Away with you, she said. —And paint her well. But don't tell her you were talking to me.

—I will not say, said Adam.

—Good man.

She sighed, and tried to smile.

—She's all I've left, she said.

Adam walked to the center of the city. He bought the paints he wanted, and a box of eggs. He also bought a hammer and a bag of steel tacks. That night, he ate all six of the eggs, fried first to safe hardness. He waited until it was dark and very quiet. Then he went out, with the hammer. There were many FOR SALE signs along the street. Adam stole only two of them. It had been raining all day, so he pulled the signs easily from the ground, as if they were onions. He dragged them quickly back to his flat, and met his neighbor, the heroin addict, at the door.

—Making a fire, bud?

—No, said Adam.

—Cool, said his neighbor.

Adam now saw something that interested him, in his neighbor's hand.

—Is that sack made of canvas? Adam asked.

—Yeah.

—You will sell it? To me?

—It has all my stuff in it.

—You will not sell it?

—Twenty euros, said his neighbor. —It's a good sack. It's probably an antique or something.

—Yes, said Adam.

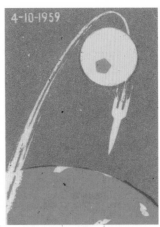

He had the correct amount in his pocket. He handed it to his neighbor. His neighbor held the sack out to Adam.

—You do not wish to empty it? said Adam.

—Hang on, said his neighbor.

He put in his hand and removed a shirt and a passport. Again, he handed the sack to Adam.

—All yours, bud.

He held up the passport.

—I'm emigrating, he said.

—To where?

—Poland, said his neighbor. —For the buzz. Good luck.

—Goodbye, said Adam.

Adam had what he needed. The oils, the canvas, and the wood. Now, he knew, he just needed the courage to gaze properly at Eve.

CHAPTER EIGHT

Adam arrived the next morning with the canvas. He had spent many hours stretching the sack and tacking it to the soft wooden legs of the FOR SALE signs.

—Cool, said Eve.

She stared at the canvas.

—It all starts today, yeah?

Adam didn't answer. He put the canvas in a corner of the kitchen and, from then on, ignored it. He also tried to ignore the smell of Eve's latest breakfast.

She sat in her allotted place. She looked at the canvas. She looked at Adam.

—Well? she said.

But Adam didn't answer. He drew.

—Cat got your tongue? she said.

He looked at Eve; he looked down. He did not know why she spoke about cats and tongues. Today he sketched no rabbits, pigs, or carrots. He drew only Eve. Her boot, her leg, a knee. He wondered where the grandmother was,

if she was nearby, listening, or even watching.

—When do you start the painting? Eve asked.

—When I am prepared, said Adam.

Another knee, her hand on the knee, an arm.

—When will that be?

—I will know, said Adam.

He liked his answer. He had not planned it.

His pencil climbed further up this woman's body. He avoided her breasts—for now; a clever trick, he thought—and drew her neck. He looked at her neck. He drew more of her neck.

—What part of Poland do you come from? she asked.

He looked at her, surprised.

—You know Poland?

—No, she said. —Not really. It's near Russia, isn't it?

Adam nodded. He concentrated on the neck.

—So, where?

—What?

—Where are you from?

—Bialystok, said Adam.

She repeated the name—she laughed.

—It sounds brilliant, she said.

—It is not so very brilliant, said Adam.

—Suit yourself, said Eve.

Adam looked at her.

—Will I shut up? she said.

No, he thought.

—Yes.

And so it progressed, until Eve stood up suddenly and said her legs were killing her. Adam took the canvas with him, and brought it back the next day.

He looked at Eve's neck, then her face. He drew. He wondered where the grandmother was. He heard no noise from any other room.

—Did you come to Ireland on your own? Eve asked.

Adam didn't answer.

—No girlfriend, no?

Adam didn't answer.

—Oh, said Eve. —He's mysterious.

—Not so very mysterious.

—Are you gay?

—No, said Adam.

He didn't blush. This pleased him, because it was a very new and unexpected question.

—There are not so many gay men in Poland, he said.

—They're all here, she said.

—Perhaps, said Adam.

He looked at her face. She looked back. He could look straight at her. This was a good day. He drew, and soon her face was below him, on the page.

This time Adam was the one to stand up.

—Tomorrow? said Eve.

—Yes, said Adam.

But he stayed away the next day. He ate two eggs, and sat on his bed for several hours. He wanted to go to Eve's house. But he also wanted to remain mysterious. "He's mysterious," Eve had said. And, Adam thought, there was nothing more mysterious than absence. So he sat on the bed until midday. Then he walked to the center of the city and bought a can of white emulsion.

The following day, Eve noticed, the canvas looked different.

—It's white, she said.

—It is emulsion, said Adam.

—What's it for? Eve asked.

—It is necessary, said Adam.

—Oh, she said. —Fine. You're the boss.

—Yes.

He put the canvas on the floor and, once again, drew Eve. He looked, and looked down at his previous sketch. He looked again at Eve. She seemed different, somehow. There was more of her. She occupied more space—Adam wasn't sure.

What he was sure about was that he loved her. He could look at her and know it. She was calm, serene. Even when she suddenly jumped, as she did now, very suddenly, he loved her.

She charged to the refrigerator.

—Put your pencil away, she said. —I'm starving.

He watched her slam the fridge door. He watched her slam the pan onto the hob. He watched her smash the eggs and slap the bacon onto the pan. He suddenly knew—he even loved her noise. He watched, and listened to her eat. He was very hungry, but this too he liked. She stuffed herself while he starved. This made Adam feel noble.

But also very hungry, and weak.

He stood up.

—Tomorrow, he said. —I will paint.

—Cool.

—Goodbye.

—Yeah, bye.

In the dark hall, as he passed the stairs, a hand came from between two rails and grabbed Adam's arm. He jumped, but did not shout.

It was the old woman, Eve's grandmother. She held a €50 note.

—Good work, she said, softly. —Take it. Buy yourself a lot more eggs.

CHAPTER NINE

Adam used a knife. He knew it was interesting.

—Where's your brush? Eve asked.

Adam didn't answer. He spread some black across the canvas.

—You're supposed to be painting me, said Eve.

—Yes.

Adam loved the near-solidity of oil.

The canvas was on a chair. He leaned down and added black to the black already there—Eve's first boot.

—What are you doing with the knife?

—Painting, said Adam.

—With a knife?

—Yes.

—Cool. My face?

—No.

—What?

He didn't answer. He squeezed more black from the tube straight onto the blade. Her boots and all her clothes were black. Adam would be using many tubes of black.

—Why do you use a knife?

—It is better, said Adam.

—How?

He shrugged. He didn't look at her. Oil paint was like reality melted, ready to solidify and become real again. With the knife, Adam felt, he didn't paint: he built. The canvas was his foundation, the oil paints were his bricks.

—I cannot explain, he said.

He built the first black boot. He didn't have a palette knife. He used the knife that had cut his eggs that morning.

He stood back. He studied what he had done. He was satisfied. It would soon be a boot; it would be a beautiful boot.

He looked quickly at the beautiful woman.

—How's it going? she asked.

—Very good, said Adam.

—Can I see?

—No.

—Go on.

—No.

Adam took the canvas home that day and brought it back the next day, and the next and next. He slowly built the picture of Eve. He had sketched her onto the white emulsion. The pencil lines disappeared beneath the oil.

He took his time. He worked slowly, deliberately. He dreaded finishing. He loved this woman and her questions. He dreaded walking out the door for the final time, without the canvas.

In the second week, he noticed something strange. He looked at Eve. He looked down at the canvas, at the remaining pencil lines. He looked again at Eve.

She saw him looking.

—What?

—Nothing, said Adam.

She was different. She was bigger.

He looked again. He wondered if love, perhaps, had made him blind, or if love, at least, had made her somewhat skinnier.

—Is something wrong?

—No, said Adam.

He flicked through his sketches.

—Did you make a mistake? she asked.

—No, said Adam. —I made no mistake.

She'd been thinner. Even three weeks before—she'd been significantly thinner. She'd put on weight; she was definitely a bigger woman. And Adam was delighted. More paint would be needed, more time—this job could go on forever.

He picked up his knife.

—I'm starving, said Eve.

Adam smiled.

—Eat, he said.

Now she looked carefully at him.

—That's nearly the first time I've seen you smile, she said. —You're a bit of a serious head.

She smiled.

—It's nice.

And he smiled—he could smile, straight at her.

—Thank you.

He met the grandmother on the street. She was carrying two full Tesco bags. She put them down, and gave him €50.

—You'll be needing more paint, she said.

She lifted the bags.

—She's a fine girl, she said. —I can't keep her fed.

She looked at him.

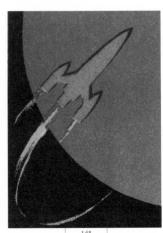

—She's happy.

Adam watched her struggle up the street, her back so low between the bags that they looked like two dark Tesco wings.

He bought more oils but, sadly, Eve had stopped expanding. She stayed within Adam's latest pencil lines. His work would soon be done. He loved her more now than he had when he'd first seen her. She was, as the old lady had said, a fine girl. He wished he could tell her that. He wished he could hold her. She was perfect, gorgeous, solid, like a distant mountain range.

But he didn't tell her anything.

He couldn't. The opportunity, his short burst of confidence, had gone. He couldn't make his mouth open. She grew distracted, bored. She stood up, she yawned, she stopped asking questions. Two days in a row she didn't open the door when he rang the bell. He knew he had to finish. He had to let her see the painting, before she stopped caring that there was a painting. Then, as she looked at herself and—Adam hoped—loved what she was seeing, then he would speak. Then he would tell her he loved her or, at least, ask her to go with him to Cineworld.

He finished the painting alone, in his room.

He rang the doorbell.

She answered.

—I'm kind of busy, she said.

—I am finished, said Adam.

—Cool, she said. —Let's see.

He leaned the canvas against the back of one of the chairs. He lifted the cover. She stared at it. He waited.

—Wow, she said. —I'm bloody gorgeous.

CHAPTER TEN

Eve was smiling now, still looking at the painting, at herself made from the oils.

—I really am something, she said.

She looked at him, for confirmation.

—Amn't I? she said. It wasn't really a question.

—Of course, said Adam.

He made himself smile, but Eve was looking at the painting again.

—I mean, she said. —I'd fall in love with me if I wasn't, you know, me already.

She leaned down.

—Is it safe to touch? she asked. —It's not wet, is it?

—No, said Adam. —You can touch.

He watched her—and he was sure he felt her, too—as she gently ran her fingers across the hills of oil, and the grooves and cuts, the various blacks, her boots, her dress, her hair, and the lighter colors, too, her neck, hands, the shaded light of the window behind her on the canvas.

She giggled—that was the word.

—Amazing, she said.

Then she walked out of the room.

Adam stayed where he was for some minutes—for half an hour. But Eve did not return. He closed the front door quietly. He'd left the painting in the kitchen.

It was over.

Two days later, as he came out of the Centra, where he'd bought six eggs and a can of spaghetti hoops, Adam met the old lady, Eve's grandmother. Her eyes were on the ground but she stopped right in front of him, as if she'd been waiting.

—Men are fools, she said. —I was hoping you'd be different. But you gave up.

Adam could think of nothing to say, except—

—Yes. It is true.

She was finished with him. She started to move. He watched her struggle into the Centra, and then walked home to his room.

He got a job he didn't like at first but which suited him quite well. He worked in a large supermarket—or, behind the supermarket, in the giant freezer, among towers of pizzas and frozen vegetables. The work was not too taxing and, because of the constant cold, Adam rarely felt that he was wasting his time. In fact, time—and life—stayed still while he was working. So it seemed to Adam. Life started again after work, when he hung up his padded jacket and stepped out of the freezer and

walked home, in late sunshine or heavy rain—it didn't matter. He felt himself come to life; the warmth crackled and became excitement. His real life started when he reached his street and his room.

Adam stood at his window every night and looked out at the street and the bare trees, and waited for Eve. When Adam fell in love he stayed in love. He couldn't help it. He was still in love with his first girlfriend, although it was more than fifteen years since he'd seen her. He was still in love with his first school-teacher, a woman who, unknown to Adam, was buried in a graveyard in Bialystok. Adam was in love with seven women. But one of them was dead and five were far away. Eve was the newest, the most urgent, and she was in Dublin, on the same street as Adam. *You gave up*, the old lady had said. She'd been right. But all winter, Adam waited.

One evening, he saw her. At last—it was her. She'd changed, but it was Eve. He watched her walk beneath the trees and streetlights. He heard her heels on the path.

She had changed.

She passed below his window.

She'd grown again—that was it—there was even more of Eve. She was bigger, more spectacular than ever. One glimpse—he saw her face just once before she walked back into darkness. She looked unhappy.

The following night, after midnight, Adam put on his jacket and a woolen cap. He put the items he needed into his pockets and left his room.

He walked past Eve's house. There were no lights on at the front of the house. He counted the number of houses to the lane—seven. He walked down the lane. It was dark here, but Adam could see his way to the next lane, even darker, which ran behind the houses. He counted the gates—seven—and stopped.

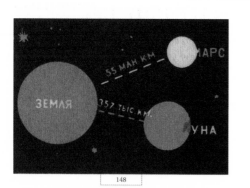

The gate was locked. The wall was high, but not very high. Adam jumped. He held on to the wall and pulled himself up. He looked at the row of houses. Some lights were on; most were off. He saw alarm-system boxes on walls, red lights blinking. There was no box on Eve's wall. Her house had no alarm.

He dropped into the garden. He walked,

hunched—he felt the wet grass soak his socks and trousers. He reached the kitchen door. It was locked. He climbed onto the narrow windowsill. He saw it quickly—the window was closed but it wasn't locked.

He lifted the window. It creaked. He listened. He dropped—he slid—into the kitchen.

CHAPTER ELEVEN

The blind was up, so it wasn't totally dark. He could see the door to the hall. He could see the fridge. He could see the table and chairs.

But he couldn't see the painting. And that was why he was there, breaking into a house he had no wish to rob. He wanted to see the painting.

He moved—two steps. He stopped. He listened. He moved again. He looked at the walls before he went out to the hall—no paintings. The hall—three paintings, but not his one. He slowly, slowly pushed open a door. He heard its creak—he felt it shiver up his arm. He stopped—he listened. He went into the room. He looked at the walls. He hoped, he prayed. But the painting wasn't there.

It wasn't on any wall downstairs.

He climbed the stairs. He heard his breath. He reached the first landing, the bathroom. No painting. He climbed higher, into the dark. The second landing, and two closed doors. Bedroom doors. He stared at these doors, Eve's and her grandmother's—and then he saw the painting. On the wall, between the doors.

His throat was dry and hurting. His heart was huge and very raw. His brain was telling him to run—*Run, run, run!*—in very urgent English.

Adam stood, and looked at the painting, at Eve, on the wall. There was a small window. Adam slowly—carefully, carefully—pulled back the curtain. He had some light now, from the street.

He—slowly, carefully—opened his jacket. The zip cracked and exploded. He stood still—*run!* He listened—*run, for God's sake!* He heard nothing—*run!*

He took his knife from his inner pocket. He took out the tube of black oil. He unscrewed the cap. He pierced the foil lid. He carefully

squeezed the tube. The smell was sudden and overpowering; it would slide in under the bedroom doors.

Adam waited.

Then he painted. In the broken light that made it through the trees, he added to Eve. He brought her up to date.

An hour later, he lay on his bed, exhausted but wide awake. He was smiling, in Polish.

The following evening, when he came home from work, he opened the door to his room and saw a €50 note on the floor, at his feet. He picked it up. He went to the window.

Every night, for hours, he stood at the window. But he had to wait some weeks before he saw Eve again. Then he did see her, suddenly, as she passed below the still-bare trees. She was walking slowly. She looked down at the ground as she moved. But he couldn't see her face. Her hair was free and definitely longer.

That night Adam climbed over Eve's back wall again. Again, he broke into the house and went carefully up the stairs. This time he painted her hair.

This was Adam's life for some more months. He spent his day in the supermarket freezer, and came home to wait for Eve. He began to see her more often now. The days were longer, and Eve was getting bigger. And this delighted Adam. The more of Eve there was, the better. Every added half-kilo was a fresh opportunity, a chance to climb over the back wall and prove his undying love.

But he waited. Until he thought she looked dejected as she passed below his window.

Then he moved. He climbed over the back wall, and broke into the house. He climbed the stairs and added weight to Eve. He hoped sometimes that one of the bedroom doors would open and Eve would find him there, and he would have to speak. He even coughed once, very softly. But both doors remained shut, to Adam's relief and disappointment.

Two more times he found €50 notes waiting when he returned from work.

The trees outside had come to life. Some of them were suddenly pink, and the strong breeze swept their blossoms along the street.

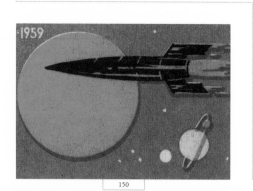

150

Adam didn't like the blossoms, any more than he had liked the falling leaves the previous autumn. They were garish and unpredictable. But then he saw Eve. She was walking under one of the blossom-shedding trees. Pink fell on black, and the blossoms were still on her shoulders and hair as she walked away from the tree. Adam held on to the windowsill.

—My God, he said—in English.

He'd never seen anything quite as beautiful in his life; this thought came in Polish. And yet, she looked unhappy. Magnificent, but very unhappy.

The following day was Adam's day off. He walked to the city center and bought a new tube of oil.

That night he climbed over the wall.

CHAPTER TWELVE

Adam crouched on top of the wall. There were lights on in the house next door. But Eve's house was dark. He let himself drop to the garden.

Once again, he climbed to the sill and opened Eve's kitchen window. Once again, he climbed into the dark kitchen.

Again, he climbed the stairs.

He stood in front of the painting and the bedroom doors. He coughed, very quietly. He waited. No sound came from either room. He took his knife from inside his jacket, and the new tube of paint. He pierced the tube. He squeezed the pink oil onto the knife. He smelled the oil in the cold air.

Minutes later, he crept back across the kitchen, to the window. He climbed onto the draining board.

—Good man.

The voice came from behind him. One of his feet was in the sink. He didn't fall—he held on to the tap. The water started running. He turned it off. His sock and trainer were soaking.

It was the old woman. But Adam couldn't see her in the dark. He climbed out of the sink, onto the floor.

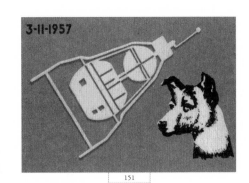

—Hello? he said.

—Don't stop for me, said the old woman. —Go on.

Adam pointed at the window.

—It is okay I go this way?

—It's lovely, said the old woman. —Go on ahead.

—Goodbye, said Adam.

—You're a good man, said the old woman; Adam still couldn't see her.

—Thank you, he said.

—She's a lucky girl, she said. —Off you go.

He climbed out the window. He went home and, eventually, he slept.

He woke—suddenly. Something had woken him. It was bright outside, behind the curtains.

—Hey!

Something hit the window, tapped it. A branch, he thought. It was windy—he could hear the gale—but the branches were not close enough to reach the glass.

—Hey!

A voice, from outside—a woman.

He was out of bed, moving to the window. He pulled back the curtain.

And the window smashed. A stone—a rock—hit Adam's chest. The broken glass and noise seemed to fill the air. Adam thought he was dead, or dying—the noise, explosion, sudden brightness. He felt glass on his feet and in his hair—his skin. He gasped—the air was dangerous, full of splinters.

But he looked out the window.

Eve was looking up at him.

—Sorry, she said.

—You broke my window, said Adam.

—You put pink spots on my painting, said Eve.

—They are blossoms, said Adam.

—I know, said Eve.

She stood in the wind, the blossoms swirling all around her.

—Come down, she said.

Adam quickly put on his jeans. He walked

across the broken glass, and down the stairs. He opened the front door. Eve stared at him. Adam looked back at her. He didn't let the wind or the blossoms distract him. He was cold, but it did not matter.

Eve spoke.

—How many times have you done it?

—What? said Adam.

—Messed with the picture, said Eve.

Adam shrugged.

—Not so many times, he said.

—And you broke into the house to do it? said Eve.

Again, Adam shrugged.

—Yes, he said.

—Jesus, said Eve. —That's amazing. You must be in love with me. Are you?

—Yes, said Adam. —That is correct.

Behind him, the door slammed shut. But he didn't look back. He didn't search his pockets for his key.

—I can't even remember your name, said Eve.

—Adam, said Adam.

—Oh yeah, said Eve. —Now I do. So, why do you love me?

—I like—

Adam looked at her feet.

—My boots? said Eve.

—They are very nice, said Adam.

—They're my granny's.

—Yes, said Adam.

—You knew?

—Yes, said Adam.

—So why didn't you fall for my granny instead?

Adam made himself look at Eve again.

—There are other things I also like, he said.

—Tell me, said Eve.

—I like your hair.

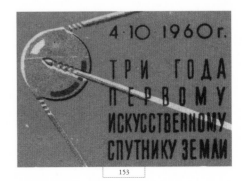

—You're bleeding, said Eve.

His face and arms had been nicked by shards of the broken glass.

—It does not matter, said Adam.

—Jesus, said Eve. —My hero. We'd better clean it up before your head goes septic, or whatever.

—I cannot go in, said Adam. —I have no key.

—Come on, said Eve.

Adam followed her, in his bare, bleeding feet, down the path, up the street, to Eve's house.

She turned to Adam before she opened her front door.

—Come here, she said.

She hugged him, for quite a while—at least twenty seconds, Adam thought. Their faces touched, and they kissed. For nine seconds.

They stopped, and Adam looked at Eve.

—You are covered in blood and blossoms, he said.

—Cool, said Eve. —I love that. Are you hungry?

—Yes, said Adam.

—Me too, she said. —I'm starving.

She held his hand.

—Come on.

Thanks to John Freeman

The Govindan Ananthanarayanan Academy for Moral and Ethical Practice and the Treatment of Sadness Resulting from the Misapplication of the Above

B E N G R E E N M A N

40 F

FELELÜNK ÉRTÜK!

The academy only lasted a decade, though the building that housed it, a former boomerang factory, still stands on the border between India and Australia. It is a modest edifice, low and long, built in 1912 by the firm of Eyre and Ananthanarayanan, which is today best known for its construction of warehouses throughout Asia but which was, at the time, interested primarily in erecting a structure for the manufacture of the company's flagship product. Parts of the factory were rebuilt several times during its first decade, but the facade has been preserved unaltered since 1920 as a result of the building's classification as a landmark. It is a somewhat interesting facade, or at the very least distinctive. There is one window shaped like a boomerang, and another shaped like the head of Markandeya, and midway between them a large iron door, above which is inscribed the official slogan of the Kaybee Karmic Boomerang Company, WE'LL KEEP YOU COMING BACK FOR MORE, which was coined by Andrew Eyre, the son of one of the founders, in 1914. Above the door on the inside are two signs, one above the other, that were installed soon after. The top sign bears a picture of a piglike man whose nose appears to be on fire. No one understands that sign. Below that, there is a sign that says HOW DO YOU FEEL WHEN THE PERSON WHO MADE YOU THE SADDEST FEELS SAD? This same question appeared, printed on a small laminated card, in selected boxes of the company's first shipment of Karmic Boomerangs, which were sent to toy stores and Hindu bookstores. Other questions in the series included, "When a Thief Is Robbed, Should You Laugh or Cry?" and "How Long Must the Good Man Wait for His Lifetime of Good Deeds to Redound to Him?" Govindan Ananthanarayanan, the son of one of the founders, composed eight of these questions in all, and affixed one to the longer arm of each Karmic Boomerang. The question above the factory door was his favorite of them. It was the one he kept coming back to—"like you might expect," he joked, to the very mild amusement of his family and colleagues—and for that reason he had it turned into a sign.

The question was interesting to Govindan mainly because he could not answer it, and the process by which he could not answer it was directly responsible for the founding of the academy that bears his name. Karmic Boomerangs, which sold slowly at first, became, in the middle years of the decade, a huge hit in both Sydney and Bombay. You could see them everywhere in public meadows and at beaches. One writer noted that "these chevrons of virtue fill the sky like a child's drawings of birds fill a child's drawings." Their vogue was short-lived, however. They were considered novelties, though Govindan Ananthanarayanan insisted that they were in fact "functioning ethical devices," and as quickly as they rose to prominence they fell away into obscurity. Both of Kaybee's founding families had made small fortunes with the ethical boomerang by then, and while the Eyres went on to become tycoons in the construction industry—taking with them the Eyre and Ananthanarayanan name, which allowed them to do business in India as well as Australia—the Ananthanarayanans, and particularly Govindan, embarked on a more scholarly course. This was not entirely surprising. Before Govindan had composed the eight questions that were packaged with the Karmic Boomerangs, he had briefly attended Oxford University (as he did again, some years later) and begun to assemble research for a thesis on James Harris Fairchild. What is not known is when, between the conversion of the company to a construction firm and Govindan's decision to reopen the factory as an academy of ethics, he chose to model his curriculum on the questions created for the boomerangs. Initially, at any rate, the curriculum was restricted to only nine courses, eight of which were based on the Kaybee cards. (The ninth was a late addition entitled, "Should You Ever Lie to a Man Who Tells You That He Has Always Told the Truth, but Whom You Suspect of Untruth?") Govindan himself taught "How Do You Feel When the Person Who Made You the Saddest Feels Sad?"

Govindan's course notes no longer exist, and as enrollment was extremely limited in those early years, we do not have any extant accounts from the perspective of students. We do, however, have a letter that Govindan wrote to a friend of his, a man named James Rouse, that deals with this same set of questions. A small amount of background is necessary. Govindan was a married man. He had, like so many young Indians, consented to an arranged marriage; his bride to be was Prabhavati Priyadarshini, a young woman whose parents were friends

of the Ananthanarayanans. The wedding took place in 1922, and accounts of it suggest that it was generally happy. Three years earlier, though, when Govindan was first informed of the match, he rebelled, insistent that he be allowed to find his own partner. Shortly after, in the summer of 1920, while studying once again at Oxford, he took notice of a young Englishwoman, Louisa Pelham. She was nineteen at the time. Govindan and Louisa embarked on a short and rocky romance that summer, and when he returned to Bombay that fall, he announced to his father that he would not marry Priyadarshini. The family refused to recognize Gonvindan's refusal. The next summer, Govindan returned to Oxford, only to find that Louisa had agreed to marry another man. Throughout that winter, while readying the academy, he expressed his suffering in a series of letters to Rouse, an Englishman he had befriended who was also close friends with Andrew Eyre. Most of the letters between Govindan and Rouse have been lost. This letter survives: in it, Govindan reacts to the news that Louisa's marriage is an unhappy one, and addresses the same question that would become the focus of his course at the academy.

> *Dear Jim,*
>
> *I received a letter from Louisa last week in which she was entirely despondent. Now and again a line would be smudged as a result of what I assume were her tears falling onto the page. The reasons, as I know you know, have to do with her marriage to Bartlett, and his treatment of her, which I am sure that you would call "beastly." I can see you saying that precise word and shaking your head uncomprehendingly. Your failure to understand human cruelty is one of the most worthy things about you.*
>
> *I have, though, a separate issue to confront. As I am sure you remember, Louisa, after taking me higher than a woman has any right to take a man, brought me lower than I thought I could go in this lifetime. It felt like I would have to ascend at least a few levels just to reach the sadness of death. It was hardly malicious on her part—after all, I was arranged to marry another woman—but it still, at the time, felt like I had been run through with a sword. There were mornings that I could not stand.*

Last week, when I received her letter, and discovered within a few sentences that she was writing from a place of great sadness, I wondered how I should feel. I mean this exactly as I have said it. I did not know how to feel. We all know about the German notion of Schadenfreude, or the Scots Gaelic aighear millteach, or the Hungarian káröröm, but those define a class of reactions to the general sufferings of others. Here, as I often have before, I am wondering about how to react to the sadness of those who cause you sadness. I would have thought that there was something in Louisa's letter that would give me, at least for a moment, a kind of joy. She had spurned me, in a sense, and the choice she made elsewhere had turned out to be a bad one. Some would say it serves her right. But then I started thinking of the times that I would sit with her in the garden, or take walks with her, and the light that would stream from her eyes as she described the type of woman she wished to become in the world. The more vividly I remembered her presence, the more crushed I was to think that any part of that light has been extinguished by fear, exhaustion, or a sense of failure. It would be melodramatic to say that I cried her tears, but inaccurate to claim that they did not at least sting my eyes and make them water.

And yet, there is a countermovement. Does she want my sadness? Is there not some danger of her feeling it as pity, or as an attempt to regain the power and control I lost when she turned me out romantically? Perhaps I am not the right person to feel sad for her. Perhaps disinterest, while impossible, would be more appropriate. I do not know exactly, Jim, but I welcome your thoughts on the matter.

Yours,
Govindan

Rouse's reply has survived.

My Dearest Govindan,

Your question is a hard one, which is why I am making no attempt to answer it.

My thoughts on the matter are the same as usual—I feel like fitting you for a priest's collar and then pulling it tight around your neck until you are dead. It would be a merciful act, my friend, as you have rarely shown even the slightest inclination toward existing

in the moment or on this good green earth, where blood courses through bodies until it finds expression in unmentionable articulations. Your head is in the clouds, as they say, and clouds are in your head. Down here on the ground, we live not by ideas but by impulses and consequences. For my part, I recently put a bun in the oven of a lovely little Belgian nurse. She is carrying high and believes that it will be a boy. Can I trouble you for a few Karmic Boomerangs? They are no longer available at toy shops or Hindu bookstores here in London, but I think the little nipper would enjoy them.

Love to Prabhavati,

Jim

Rouse did not take delivery of the boomerangs. This can be determined from the employment records at the academy, which show that only six months after this exchange, Rouse arrived to assume the duties of grounds manager and rugby coach, which had previously been performed by Andrew Eyre, who had departed for America. Rouse came without his Belgian girlfriend or his son. A note that Eyre wrote to Govindan at that time elaborates on the circumstances that brought Rouse to the academy. It is significantly more telegraphic than the other men's letters: "Jim," Eyre writes, "ran. I understand. Found out that the child wasn't his, decided to stay and do his part. Passed through a change. Became changed man. Then found out that the child was his after all. Some men would have been happy. Jim reasoned that any woman who would have been willing to have another man's child was—well, Jim ran. Hope he's good for rugby." In fact, during Rouse's time there, the institution earned far more renown for its athletics than it did for its moral and ethical instruction. The teams, whether in rugby or football, were extremely competitive, almost martial, and showed little mercy for opponents. Eventually, the marked contrast between the comportment of students in the classroom and on the field became central to the curriculum. One course dealing with the issue, taught by Govindan in 1929, was called "If You Destroy an Opponent, Should You Be Eternally Worried That Your Opponent Will One Day Return to Destroy You?" It is rumored, but cannot be proven, that Rouse sat in on the class.

The academy was shuttered in 1931, after a protracted lawsuit brought by the father of a former student who was injured during a rugby match; it was suggested that Rouse's style of coaching led directly to the injury. All of the academy's remaining assets, including several dozen cases of boomerangs, were sold off to pay the settlement, as was the building itself, which became a community center and a museum dedicated to the history of the transcontinental border. Govindan, who had managed not to lose any of his personal wealth, moved to Sydney with his family—and Rouse, still single, came along. In Sydney, two months later, out walking along the waterfront and back, Govindan Ananthanarayanan encountered Louisa Pelham Bartlett, who had come to Australia after the death of her husband. The two of them resumed a friendship, and Govindan encouraged her to strike up a relationship with Rouse, who was occupying a small apartment in the back house of the Ananthanarayanan estate. "I know that this makes no sense to you, because it makes no sense to me," he wrote to Eyre in 1933, "but I want to keep her near me, and I am hoping that if she takes up with Rouse that it will achieve the desired effect. Desired effect: that is far too neutral and scientific a phrase for the almost childish joy I am hoping I might one day feel." It was not to be. Rouse was, by this time, a hard man, impossible to reason with, let alone love, and whether or not he sensed Govindan's true intentions, he proved to be a poor collaborator. For two months, he inserted himself as a blunt obstruction between Govindan and Pelham Bartlett, and his abrasive manner ultimately drove her away from the Ananthanarayanan family. More to the point, it drove her out of Australia; she soon married an American businessman, who then moved to Kyoto. Rouse insisted

that Pelham Bartlett's departure did not bother him, as he had felt nothing for the woman when she was present. Nevertheless, he was keenly aware that his friend was suffering from her absence all over again, and this brought on a nervous breakdown that landed Rouse in Sacred Heart Hospital. "You didn't want her around anyway," Rouse wrote to Govindan from the hospital. "She had harmed you. Don't you remember? Why would you want to keep ties with someone like that? I must confess I don't understand you. But I am sorry if I have harmed you." After six months, Rouse was released, and he returned to the Ananthanarayanan home, where he began to work as a driver for the family. When Rouse heard in 1940 that the mother of his child had died in a car accident, he was at the horse track with Govindan Ananthanarayanan. "A driver killed her?" Rouse reportedly said. "That evens the score." He took off his driver's cap, placed it over his heart, and lowered his head. "My failure to understand human cruelty," he said, and began to laugh.

Cadence

ERICA PLOUFFE LAZURE

Something ate a hole through the oil tank, so we called Joey in from the pumps to fix it. The tank had been drained, mostly, but mostly never helped no one. Joey didn't have gloves, just some rubber goggles, and this one time nobody told him to go and get the good mask. He could've found the cat litter in the closet, could've poured it in first to absorb what we'd left in there, but he didn't do that either. It probably wouldn't have helped. Even with those goggles on he would've seen the ember that strayed through the hole, the welding rod still pinched between his fingers, the little spark that built the flame that rocked us all to the back of the bay.

The body looks strange on fire. It's just everywhere at once, liquid and growing, Joey tearing out toward the nasty patch of grass on Highway 11 with flames eating through his skin. And we just stood there stupid, like disciples struck, helpless except for a woman waiting for an oil change who called 911 from our pay phone. But what were we supposed to do? He was gone, and we all knew it, except maybe for Mr. Arlen, moving too late from behind his desk, belly-heavy in work boots, extinguisher in hand. The fire was out already. Joey was blind and smoldering with snuffed heat on that small strip of highway lawn, me kneeling nearby telling him the things he'd want to hear in his last few moments, cars still pulling into the station. And Mr. Goddamn Fucking Hero Arlen pushing through with his cherry-red tank, the pin pulled—it made me wish, as the foam hit and Joey screamed his last, that Mr. Arlen had stayed behind his goddamned desk. He stood over Joey holding the tank like he'd just taken the world's biggest pressurized piss. That's when I threw up.

In all the years I knew him, Joey was never one to just let a subject be. And for the past month he'd been nonstop about his girl Becky in Basic. When she left for the Army he went on and on about the mix tape he'd made for her, the magazines he'd bought her, the fudge his mother made, the jumbo pack of Skittles he'd found at

Sam's Club, the troll doll with camouflage hair and pants to match. He liked to tell me all about her "particular brand of fucking," as he'd called it, specialty moves of hers that I knew only too well. So well that I knew when he started to make stuff up. He didn't write many letters; he was more of a candy-and-flowers man. He'd sit at the station between pump calls and write a few I-miss-you's on yellow lined paper. And just last week he told me how the Skittles and the fudge and the mix tape and the rest of it was banned anyway.

"What she got," he said, "was one good look at all the things I'd sent her. Then her sergeant took it all away. Worse than me not sending it at all."

Becky has good features but bad skin that she tries to hide with beige makeup. She keeps at least three bottles of that stuff in her bathroom. I've seen it. *Contour*, she calls it. It works better at night, or in the dark, at bars a few towns over. Becky's barroom eyeliner makes you forget about those bottles of pancake in her bathroom, makes you forget how a close hug from her will more than likely leave a tan rash on your T-shirt. A few years back she was co-captain superstar forward of the Lady Tigers, the kid-sister legacy to All-State field-hockey champs Bunny and Boli Barker.

But the first time Becky took me home from Duck's Tavern she was already over all that. She had a thread of green dental floss strung across her left breast, stuck to the nubs of her sweater, clinging like tinsel to the pilled part below her shoulder, and she gave me one of those hidden, rim-of-the-eye smiles when I asked about her hygiene technique. "Gotta keep the girls plaque-free somehow," she said. She told me she'd started young in the bars, nabbing one of her big sisters' IDs when she was seventeen. No one ever called her on it, even though her picture was in all the papers that season. Ask me, that four-year jump-start on bar life kept with her and there she was at twenty-four at the same bar looking at least thirty under all that makeup.

Becky's been writing to me since her first week at Basic, saying from the start how she wished she'd wrapped it up with Joey before she left. How she wants me instead of him. How the one thing Basic fails to train you for is what to do with the life you leave back in Mewborn. Last week she said Joey had one more letter coming, and then she'd be free for me, for real. She told me to watch for it, made me promise to talk to him if he brought it up. She said, "My sergeant says, 'The more you carry, the more you carry.' I don't have room for a troll doll, anyway."

And so I wasted the whole morning looking for clues in his face. At Burger King I waited for him to say something about her, because that was my cue, my lead-in to let him know his personal business with Becky was mine, too. I could see the folded note in the pocket of his T-shirt, the telltale border on the envelope. But he just ate his burger with fries and talked about Friday's game at the high school like nothing had changed, like Becky was still scoring points in her plaid skirt and mouth guard. I waited for it all day and he said not a word, not a word until the spark hit that puddle of oil. Not until he was down on the ground with no face, me kneeling next to him—that's when he talked, right before Arlen came barreling through with his goddamn superman extinguisher. I heard him.

Becky's got a month left of Basic, and then it's off to Aberdeen for ordnance training. Between the training is two weeks at home. She's thinking about going Airborne so she can nab a Fort Bragg assignment, so there'd be but an hour between us. She picked ordnance, she said, because she loves dogs, even the bomb-sniffing ones. She's hinted more than once I should think about a move to Fayetteville, right by Bragg. Even though she's in South Carolina and on her way to Maryland. Even though it's the Bragg soldiers they're shipping daily overseas. Even though I wasn't sure I wanted Becky in-the-daylight. Becky out-of-bars. Becky out-of-bed. I wrote her as much using nicer words, said I wasn't sure I was worth jumping out of a plane for. But I said I'd talk to Joey if she talked to him first.

But then Joey died. I saw him tear across our lot with the welder still on. The oil tank scattered across the bay in white-hot pieces. Bits of it kicked into his skin, turned him to blue flame in seconds. He cooked the palms of his hands trying to pry the goggles from his face.

The rules change after a fuel tank explodes and eyelids burn away and tear ducts are gone and you're kneeling beside your best friend and his face and body have no skin. Becky would understand. In Basic they tell each other stories that end like this, best friends and fire and all. Knowing her, she'll listen to every

track on that tape Joey made. She'll make me come pick her up at Fort Jackson and I'll have to hear it all the way home. And at some point, she'll loosen my grip from the stick shift and hold my hand in her lap and won't say a thing about what happened. She'll collar me with her silence and grief and guilt as "Tumbling Dice" moves through us, and that's when I'll know that I'm hers now, that this is the way she'll pull us into public. At Joey's funeral they'll play "I'll Be There for You" straight from the tape and she'll appear in her dress uniform and claim her place as Grieving Girlfriend, and I'll be the Grieving Best Friend and his parents will be real nice to both of us and won't it make sense to everyone for us to find comfort together in our loss? It's just what he would have wanted, she'll say, me finishing with her what Joey could not. And how cheap would it be to tell her what a farce that mix tape really is, how Joey borrowed more than half my tape collection and then used my boom box to make it? It's not worth upstaging someone after they're dead.

Which is why she won't ask what we talked about. Which is why I won't tell her that when I knelt by Joey and told him about Becky in her boots, marching across a swamp in South Carolina, clutching a map, finding a coordinate, on her way back to him, Arlen almost there with the extinguisher, I swear I heard him say it. "I know," he said. "I know."

And what do *I* know? It was nobody's fault. Even when I thought about what might happen down the line, to her out there and Joey here and me in between, I saw it all working itself out. I didn't see myself looking at what's left of Joey. I didn't see me losing him and her getting me. I still don't see it.

Calls

YANNICK MURPHY

ГУСИ-ЛЕБЕДИ

CALL: A cow with her calf half born.

ACTION: Put on boots and pulled calf out while standing in a field full of mud.

RESULT: Tore hind legs off from calf. Head, forelegs, and torso are still inside the mother.

THOUGHTS ON DRIVE HOME: Is there a nicer place to live?

WHAT THE CHILDREN SAID TO ME WHEN I GOT HOME: Hi, Pop.

WHAT THE WIFE COOKED FOR DINNER: Something mixed up.

CALL: Old woman with minis needs bute paste.

ACTION: Drove to old woman's house, delivered bute paste. Petted minis. Learned their names: Molly, Netty, Sunny, and Storm.

RESULT: Minis are really cute.

THOUGHTS ON DRIVE HOME: Must bring children back here sometime to see the cute minis.

WHAT THE CHILDREN SAID TO ME WHEN I GOT HOME: Hi, Pop.

WHAT THE WIFE COOKED FOR DINNER: Steak and potatoes.

CALL: Sick sheep.

ACTION: Visited sheep. Noticed they'd eaten all the thistle.

RESULT: Talked to owner, who is a composer, about classical music. Admired his tall barn beams. Advised owner to fence off thistle so sheep couldn't eat it. Sheep become sick from thistle.

THOUGHTS ON DRIVE HOME: Is time travel possible? Maybe time is not a thing. Because light takes a while to travel, what we're seeing is always in the past.

WHAT THE WIFE COOKED FOR DINNER: Breakfast.

CALL: Castrate draft horse.

ACTION: Pulled out emasculators, castrated draft horse.

RESULT: Draft horse bled buckets. Pooled around his hooves. Owner said she had never seen so much blood. It's okay, he's got a lot of blood, I said. She nodded. She braided the fringe on her poncho, watching the blood.

THOUGHTS ON DRIVE HOME: What's the point of a poncho if it doesn't cover your arms?

WHAT THE WIFE SAID TO THE CHILDREN WHEN I GOT HOME: Your father's home.

WHAT THE WIFE COOKED FOR DINNER: Nut loaf.

WHAT I ATE FOR DINNER: Not nut loaf.

CALL: Horse is colicking.

ACTION: Drove to horse. Gave him Banamine. Watched him rolling on his stall floor. Watched owner cry. Just a few tears down a freckled cheek. Listened to horses in other stalls whinny, worried for the colicky horse.

RESULT: Stayed for hours, until night. Moon was full. Walked horse out to field by the apple tree. Gave him a shot to put him to sleep. Patted his neck. Left owner with her head by his head, she wasn't saying anything to him. Maybe just breathing in his last exhaled breath.

THOUGHTS ON DRIVE HOME: When I go I want to go in a field by an apple tree on a full-moon night.

WHAT I SAW WHEN I PULLED UP TO THE HOUSE: Bright lights in the sky, an object moving quickly back and forth. Not a plane.

WHAT I HEARD FROM THE CHILDREN WHEN I GOT HOME: Gentle snoring.

WHAT I HEARD FROM MY WIFE WHEN I GOT HOME: Loud snoring.

CALL: Sheep with a cut from a fence.

ACTION: Drove to farm. Inspected sheep. Cut was old. Small white worms were crawling on it. Gave owner some antibiotic.

RESULT: Asked owner if he had seen the bright lights in the sky the night before. Owner shrugged. I go to bed, the owner said.

THOUGHTS ON DRIVE HOME: Since people have become used

to seeing telephone wires and telephone poles everywhere, they can get used to seeing windmills everywhere. It's just a matter of getting used to something.

WHAT I SAW WHEN I PULLED UP TO THE HOUSE: The thing with bright lights in the sky.

WHAT THE CHILDREN SAID TO ME: Poppy, we're scared.

WHAT THE WIFE SAID: It must be one of those police crafts that hunts fields for marijuana.

WHAT I SAID: But we don't grow marijuana.

WHAT THE CHILDREN SAID: What's marijuana?

WHAT WE SAID: Go inside.

WHAT THE CHILDREN SAID WE ATE FOR DINNER: Moonburgers and Martian fries.

CALL: Alpaca down.

ACTION: Drove to farm. Remembered not to look alpaca in the eye.

RESULT: Looked alpaca in the eye by mistake. Got spit in the eye. Alpaca nice and angry now. Alpaca got up. Owner thankful. Handed me a rag that smelled like gasoline. Wiped my eye.

THOUGHTS ON DRIVE HOME: I could have been an engineer or a fighter pilot.

CALL: A prepurchase examination on a thoroughbred.

ACTION: Brought digital X-ray machine and performed a complete set of X-rays on horse in a barn with ducks, spaniels, and kittens walking about.

RESULT: Owner tried to give me a kitten to take home to the children. No, no, I said. We have two dogs. The dogs will love the cat, the owner said. How about a duck? the owner said. No, they shit liquid, I said. Yes, that's true, she said, but the eggs are golden.

THOUGHTS ON RIDE HOME: Chickens might be nice to have. The children could check for eggs every day. We could eat the eggs. Chickens don't shit liquid. This is the problem today, people don't know where their food comes from. My children will know where their food comes from.

WHAT I SAW WHEN I DROVE UP TO THE HOUSE: A spaceship in the field. My wife, my children inside it.

Where was dinner?

What were the children saying to me?

175

Why was my wife waving me aboard? Why were my children's mouths black holes calling my name? Were they all sick? Had they foundered? Colicked? Come up lame?

WHAT I THOUGHT: What do I have inside my truck to cure them? Bute? Banamine?

WHAT I KNEW: There is nothing inside my truck. They just want me.

Everything was talking. The trees talked. Go forward, they said. The grass spoke. Go forward, it said. My truck was a regular Chatty Cathy. Go on, go on, it said.

WHAT THE SPACESHIP SAID: Come aboard.

ACTION: I climbed aboard.

WHAT THE SPACESHIP SMELLED LIKE: Cinnamon.

WHAT THE CHILDREN SAID: Watch this.

WHAT MY WIFE DID: Pressed a button.

RESULT: We took off. We sailed into the sky. I looked down out the windows. I could see all the houses in our town. I could see the old woman with the minis. Molly, Netty, Sunny, and Storm were nibbling grass. They were so tiny, they looked like brown children on all fours. There are the minis I wanted you to see, I said to the children. Then I could see the winding stream and the pond where my son had once caught a large trout and the rest of us caught trout as small as our hands. There is no nicer place to live. I saw Bill, the owner of the general store, he was shoveling the snow from his steps. I waved. There's Bill, the children said. They waved too and knocked on the spaceship glass. Bill did not look up. There was a lot of snow so I can see why he didn't look up. He had a job to do.

БЫЧОК-ЧЁРНЫЙ БОЧОК, БЕЛЫЕ КОПЫТЦА

BRIAN BAISE lives in Somerville, Massachusetts. His fiction has also appeared in the *St. Anne's Review.*

RODDY DOYLE's latest books are *The Deportees* and, for younger readers, *Wilderness.* He lives and sometimes works in Dublin.

BLAZE GINSBERG was born in Portland, Oregon, and grew up in San Diego, California. He has been writing songs, stories, and poems since he was nine years old.

BEN GREENMAN is an editor at the *New Yorker* and the author of several books of fiction, including *Superbad, Superworse, A Circle Is a Balloon and Compass Both,* and the forthcoming *Please Step Back.* "The Govindan Ananthanarayanan Academy..." is from the forthcoming collection *Correspondences.* He lives in Brooklyn.

LAURA HENDRIX studied at the University of Alabama; she now works as a school librarian. Her work has been published in the *Mid-American Review.*

ERICA PLOUFFE LAZURE is a writer and musician living in Greenville, North Carolina. Her fiction has appeared in the *North Carolina Literary Review, Smokelong Quarterly,* and the *Mad Hatters' Review.*

NATHANIEL MINTON's fiction has appeared in previous issues of *McSweeney's,* as well as in *ZYZZYVA, Dustup,* and elsewhere. He is currently attending the Iowa Writers' Workshop, where he is a Teaching-Writing Fellow.

YANNICK MURPHY is the author of the novels *Signed, Mata Hari, Here They Come,* and *The Sea of Trees.* She has also published two short story collections, *In a Bear's Eye* and *Stories in Another Language.*

JOYCE CAROL OATES is the author, most recently, of the story collection *Wild Nights!* and the novel *My Sister, My Love: The Intimate Story of Skyler Rampike.* She lives and teaches in Princeton, New Jersey.

PETER ORNER is the author of a novel, *The Second Coming of Mavala Shikongo,* and a short-fiction collection, *Esther Stories*. He is also the editor of a recently published book of oral histories, *Underground America: Narratives of Undocumented Lives*. He lives in San Francisco.

NELLY REIFLER is the author of *See Through*, a collection of stories. Her fiction has appeared in many journals and magazines in the United States and abroad. She lives in Saugerties, New York.

DAWN RYAN is a writer from Massachusetts, currently living in New Jersey and attending the Rutgers-Newark MFA program. Her piece "E Pluribus Unum" can be found online at the *Raleigh Quarterly*.

J. ERIN SWEENEY is the author of one novel, *Century Farm*, and a collection of short stories. Her work has appeared in various literary journals, and been performed on stage in Philadelphia, Atlanta, and New York. She lives and works in Philadelphia.

JOHN THORSON lives in Vermont. "Following a Lifetime of Fabrication…" is his first story to appear in print.